William Branks

Life in Heaven

SALZWASSER
VERLAG

William Branks

Life in Heaven

Reprint of the original, first published in 1863.

1st Edition 2022 | ISBN: 978-3-37500-107-0

Verlag (Publisher): Salzwasser Verlag GmbH, Zeilweg 44, 60439 Frankfurt, Deutschland
Vertretungsberechtigt (Authorized to represent): E. Roepke, Zeilweg 44, 60439 Frankfurt, Deutschland
Druck (Print): Books on Demand GmbH, In de Tarpen 42, 22848 Norderstedt, Deutschland

LIFE IN HEAVEN.

THERE, FAITH IS CHANGED INTO SIGHT,

AND

HOPE IS PASSED INTO BLISSFUL FRUITION.

BY THE AUTHOR OF

"HEAVEN OUR HOME," AND "MEET FOR HEAVEN."

EDINBURGH

1863.

PREFACE.

THE great and unlooked-for success which has attended the publication of my two preceding volumes, "Heaven our Home," and "Meet for Heaven," (their united sale having been already 75,000 copies in this country alone,) has naturally induced me to believe that my labours in the sphere of literature to which I have as yet turned my attention have not been unacceptable to the public.

As there remained, however, several important elements in connexion with the same subject which were not embraced in the two books above mentioned, and which, I conceive, are of still greater interest to my readers than the views previously presented, I resolved to complete my efforts in this particular department of literature by a new volume.

I have accordingly prepared this work in the hope that it may contribute likewise in some degree to maintain an interest in the momentous subject of which it treats.

CONTENTS.

"YOUR LIFE IS HID WITH
CHRIST IN GOD."

CHAPTER I.

THE EARTH NOT THE HOME IN WHICH WE ARE TO LIVE FOR EVER.

EVEN were we to remain upon the earth as long as it shall exist, still there is a day coming when the earth itself will be among the things that were. "The day of the Lord will come as a thief in the night; in the which the heavens shall pass away with a great noise, and the elements shall melt with fervent heat, the earth also and the works that are therein shall be burned up. Seeing, then, that all these things shall be dissolved, what manner of persons ought ye to be in all holy conversation and godliness?" The things that are to be dissolved, according to the apostle's distinct enumeration of them, are *the starry heavens, the elements, and the earth;* these are the things against which a sentence of dissolution has come out from Him who, in awful sovereignty, is seated upon the throne of the universe, who lifts up His hand, not to heaven, but above the highest heavens, and says,

I live for ever. The heavens are to be dissolved: not the third heavens, not the world of glory above, where God has His throne, into which Jesus in His glorified humanity has ascended, and in which the angels of God and the glorified members of the human family from earth have their present habitation and home with God—but the visible heavens, the sun, the planets, the stars; these are one day, like the gas-lamps throughout the streets of a city when the morning sun looks out upon its awaking inhabitants, to be blown out by the breath of Him whose omnific word gave them existence. They will one day be missed, when the inhabitants of heaven look forth and see them no longer rolling in their several orbits in which they have revolved. The elements are to be dissolved,—the visible heavens and the earth, and all that exists betwixt them. The earth itself, which for nearly six thousand years has been a habitation to the passing generations of the human family, is also to be dissolved: "The earth also, and the works that are therein, shall be burned up."

There are two diametrically opposite opinions held among Christians regarding the *nature* of the change which the last conflagration shall produce upon the material universe. Some expounders of the Bible think that when the Holy Spirit speaks in its pages about the effect of that deluge of fire, that is on the last day of this world's history to encircle the earth and envelope in its embrace the material and visible creation, that He speaks not of the *annihilation*, but of the *transformation* of the material universe. These individuals think the very *fact* that Christ himself, the Second Person of the Godhead, and the Head of the Church, has allied Himself to matter in the assumption of a real body, and has united for eternity the human nature and the divine, and has ascended in our nature to the throne of God—they think the very *fact* that Enoch and Elijah even *now* stand before God, in the court of heaven, appearing there in their glorified human bodies, resplendent and shining like Christ's own glorious body—they think the very *fact* that *the whole* of the children of God, on the resurrection morning, are to receive their bodies from Christ, when all who are in the grave shall hear His voice and come forth, and are to ascend in their upraised bodies upwards into a glorious eternity, *discountenances* the idea that there is to be the *annihilation* of matter. They think that the fire of the last conflagration is to do to the material universe what fire does to gold,—it is to melt it and purify it, in God's great crucible, that it may be thrown and cast over again into a new and a more beauteous form, so that out of the matter which at present exists, God may reconstruct the new heavens and the new earth, where righteousness, through eternity, shall have its peaceful and happy reign.

I do not agree with these views. I do not object

to them merely because they give a too dignified and unchanging and permanent view of the earth, which is our present home, but because they are in their nature and tendency *atheistical.* They involve the tacit assumption that God, by His power, can recast and remodel, but cannot *destroy* matter,—that matter possesses so inherently the element of *essential existence* that it is beyond even the prerogative of Almighty God to annihilate it. What I contend for is, *there is nothing self-existent but God.* God created matter at first out of nothing by the word of His power,—when He spoke, and it was done,—when He gave the command, and the heavens and the earth came into being. God has only to speak the word again, and the present earth and the visible material heavens will cease to be. They will be laid, if not in the grave of forgetfulness, at least in the sepulchre of non-existence and of eternal nothingness.

There are accordingly other expounders of the Bible who think, that when the Holy Spirit speaks in its pages about the *heavens* and the *elements* and the *earth being dissolved,* the words point out not the *transformation,* but the *annihilation* of matter. I believe in this opinion. I have no preconceived theory to support. I wish to sit with the docility of a little child at the feet of Jesus, and in reverence to listen to His voice whilst He describes by His Spirit, in His own blessed Word, the *change* which the last day is to bring and spread over the material universe. I feel afraid to tamper with the literalities of Scripture; and my belief is, that the language of inspiration generally, and a few graphic passages of the Bible in particular, announce, not the *transformation*, but the *annihilation* of the matter now composing God's visible, lower creation, including the earth.

All these things shall be dissolved. What possibly can mean such Scripture expressions as these but the *destruction* of matter? "All the host of heaven shall be dissolved, and the heavens shall be rolled together as a scroll: and all their host shall fall down, as the leaf falleth off from the vine, and as a falling fig from the fig-tree." "And I beheld when he had opened the sixth seal, and, lo, there was a great earthquake; and the sun became black as sackcloth of hair, and the moon became as blood; and the stars of heaven fell unto the earth, even as a fig-tree casteth her untimely figs, when she is shaken of a mighty wind." It gives to the whole intelligent population throughout God's great universe, as well as to man upon the earth, a terrible view of the *evil of sin*, when God in His Word reveals these *two facts—because of sin*, that He who is a God of love might have it in His power to pardon it, the Lord from heaven, the Son of the Highest, had to veil His splendour, and leave the glories of eternity, and come to earth, and suffer and die; and *because of sin*, the visible material universe, including the earth, our present home, is to be destroyed. This was typified among the Jews. When leprosy entered a house during the existence of the Mosaic economy, what were the Jews commanded to do? Were they merely to purify and whitewash the house, and leave it standing? No; they were enjoined to destroy the house by fire, and in the same way to consume everything that was in it.

The leprosy of sin has entered the world—and death by sin—one room of the house constituting God's visible creation; and from the language of Scripture, it appears to be God's resolution not to purify the house merely by casting sin and death out of it, and banishing them for ever into an eternity of woe, but to destroy the house altogether, and that by fire.

There is something terribly appalling, fearfully and alarmingly bewildering, in the announcement that is made by God himself from the throne of His sovereignty, that the lower creation is to be dissolved. Yon sun, that has been travelling in his pavilion of light in the face of the high and overarching sky for nearly six thousand years, is not to continue his journey there throughout the revolving cycles of the eternity that is to come; he is one day to disappear and be no more seen. The angels of God and the saints who will then be in glory, will look out from heaven and down upon the place that once formed the sun's orbit, but he will be away for ever; just as you look out upon the ocean after a storm, and no longer behold the gallant ship there, with its dark hull and its white sails outspread, for it has foundered and gone down, and has disappeared beneath the rolling waves. They will look forth and see the orbit dark and deserted along which the bright sun long travelled, whilst the poor sun himself is lying in the grave of the original nothingness out of which he arose, when at God's call he made his appearance upon the stage of existence, and took his assigned place among the works of God's hands. The maiden moon, in her quiet, pale serenity, which for nearly six thousand years has been reflecting the sun's light, and has been gliding along in her orbit through the sky amidst the music of the spheres, with all the stars around her,—that moon which has so long, to the imaginations of the poets of earth, appeared to be one of the brightest gems that gleam and sparkle upon the crown that encircles the brow of old night, will one day be looked for and anxiously inquired after by the countless assemblies who stand before the throne of God, but she will have disappeared for ever. The stars that have so long been seen by the assemblies of heaven, and by the passing generations of the human family upon earth, like so many centres of light studding in their gleaming brightness the bosom of the great ocean of space, are one day to fall from the firmament and strew the plains of annihilation. This earth, *upon* the surface of which so many of the human family are living, and *in* the bosom of which so many of the dead are sleeping, is one day to melt, dissolve, and disappear like snow from one of its mountain summits when the sudden thaw descends upon it.

And what a lofty view does it give us of God's eternity and of the unchangeableness of His sovereignty, when we think that amid all the changes that are to come down upon God's visible creation, God himself will be sitting upon the throne of His sovereignty and of His glory quite unaffected and unmoved, not suffering even the shadow of a change, whilst all that is now visible to us is passing away! The heavens are to be rolled together like a scroll, the *earth* to be burned up.

Say not, sceptic, that this cannot be! The truthful word of the Most High declares that they are scoffers who deny it. Say not that, through the eternity that is before us, no change further than a mere transformation is to pass upon the material universe. God is upon the throne of His truth as well as upon the throne of His sovereignty and of His power, and He has declared that all these things are to be dissolved. Matter, in all its ponderousness and massiveness, and endless variety of form and beauteous appearances, is lying passive and prostrate at the feet of the Almighty. God has only to speak the word, and the dissolution of the matter which composes the numberless orbs of the lower material creation will take place. God has only to give utterance to the command, and these visible heavens that are above us, and this earth that is spread with its riches around us, will disappear and return to their original nothingness. To an eye that sees at one glance the whole universe of God, the whole lower creation would, if blotted out, be missed from the universe just as little as one grain of sand would be missed from the sea-shore, or one leaf from the great and wide-spreading forest, or one drop of water from the great roll of the Atlantic Ocean, or one drop of dew from the numberless drops that glitter over the plain beneath the increasing light of the morning sun.

The luminaries of the sky have often, in our apprehension, something like the perpetuity of eternity about them, and of the stability of an endless existence. They are so unlike, in the long ages of their duration, to the lightning's gleam; the midnight meteor that flashes over the sky and disappears amid the again gathering darkness of night; the flowers, earth's fading beauties, that bud and bloom, and in a few weeks wither and die; man, whose breath is in his nostrils, who comes forth as a flower and is cut down, who flees also as a shadow, and continues not; or even the oak, that lifts its head so proudly upon the mountain's brow, and only decays, and falls, and withers, at the end of hundreds of years. These luminaries of the sky appear to us to be stable and enduring as the pillars of heaven, or rather as heaven itself, or as the very throne of God. They have remained in their appointed places since the morning of creation; they have been looking on and beholding the whole past generations of the human family, the actors in the great drama of human existence here, successively passing over the stage of time, and disappearing from the land of the living behind the curtain that hides eternity from us, to begin the actings for eternity on the other side. The same sun, the same moon, the same stars, that shed their light upon a once unfallen world, upon our first parents as they walked in their innocency, and beauty, and love, through the garden of Eden, are still shedding, in the profusion of an inexhaustible abundance, their ocean floods of light upon us who are now acting out our little day on the world's great stage, and in fulfilment of God's appointments with us here: but they are not to remain in their present spheres for ever; their change will come, and their funeral day will arrive, and their consignment to the tomb of annihilation will take place. The earth is a poor prisoner, placed for a season in the prison of God's lower creation, but the day of its execution will come, when the pall of an eternal night will descend upon it.

Meditation upon such a subject as the dissolution of the visible heavens and of the earth is not an *idle speculation*: on the contrary, it is calculated to detach our thoughts from *matter* and from *time*, and from all the *evanescent transactions* of the sublunary scene that now encircles us, and to raise them to God, to Jesus, to the Holy Spirit, and to heavenly and eternal realities. The astronomer surveys the starry firmament with his telescope, and beholds the mighty orbs which God has spread around Him in the great pavilion of space; but too often his eye fails to see in these the fringes of the bright garments of God's glory, the gleamings of the candles lighting the bright and gorgeous palace in which God Almighty walks. The geologist explores the strata and the formations and the internal appearances of the earth which God created and built; but too often, while walking to and fro in these researches, he fails to meet and to recognise God, who, in His upholding and beneficent presence, spake the earth at first into existence, and who hung it upon nothing. The mariner goes down into the great sea, he beholds the wonders of Jehovah in the mighty deep; but too often, whilst sailing upon the bosom of the mighty ocean, which is the Almighty's great mirror, he beholds not God's image reflected there, whose way is in the sea, and whose footsteps are in the mighty deep. The traveller visits different countries in succession,—he passes over the surface of this earth, which was once without form and void, with the unremoved darkness of a past eternity brooding over it, and which was, on the morning of creation, formed and fashioned and beautified by the Spirit of the Lord moving upon it,—he meets and mingles with the various tribes of men, who still, even in their fallen condition, reflect—much defaced, no doubt—the image of God; but how often does the same traveller pass up and down among the living works of God's hands, and still never, or at least but seldom, gain a glimpse of Him in His upholding presence, and in the profusion of His beneficent goodness. The material universe is the god of some individuals; the huge mass of materialism rises up before them and around them, engages all their attention, engrosses all their thoughts; and thus, in their earthly and materialised cogitations, not even one stray thought rises, as if upon the outspread wings of an eagle, upwards to Him who is seated in His sovereignty, and in all the splendour of His ineffable glory, upon the throne of heaven. The earth, with its riches and honours, with its sins and pleasures, with its friendships and loves, and with its infinitely varied occupations, is the god of others. The great material universe, which God has summoned into existence and has spread around Him, often does to the thoughts of man what a mountain or a wall or a veil does to the eye,—it intercepts the thoughts in their rising and upward flight to God, and thus shuts out of view altogether Him whom angels behold amid the light of a high and glorious eternity, whom the glorified in heaven see eye to eye, and before whom they pour forth their seraphic voices in this hallelujah acclaim, "Great and marvellous are thy works, Lord God Almighty; just and true are thy ways, thou King of saints." Oh, there are many poor, little, contracted-minded worldlings, who feel, as it were, a heavy lump of lead hung to the wing of every upward thought and of every heavenly aspiration, and who never in their contemplations rise from the view of nature, and ascend in their realising contemplations and reflections upwards to nature's God. The material universe through our sin—the great orbs of the firmament—instead of being to us as so many bright and shining mirrors reflecting the image of God's glorious presence in His eternal power and Godhead, rise up as a bright wall to conceal God from us, and thus too often become the means, through the darkness that is in us, of hiding God altogether from our view.

Are you, my readers, numbered among those to whom God's works are everything, and God himself is nothing? Are your thoughts occupied chiefly, if not exclusively, with the things of earth? Do you mind earthly things, and does your imagination never soar to the things that are above, and to the vivid realisation of the invisible, great, and eternal realities about which the Bible speaks? Is the mole boring in the earth your representative, and not the eagle in its upward flight into the pure and calm and deep serene that is above? Let me call to your remembrance the fact that the earth is not to be your dwelling-place for ever. You must soon leave it. When you are removed from it and are away, what things will then become the chief objects of your thoughts?

God is everything to those who are in a glorious eternity. He is the great and mighty and perpetual object of contemplation to those who are in heaven, who enjoy the beatific vision, however little He may be thought about by you in the midst of your present avocations and sins and pleasures. The earth is about to slip away from your embrace. "The things that are seen are temporal." What will you contemplate, and what will you think about, when the material universe has been dissolved and has disappeared from your view? Will God *then* be the supreme and fixed and rapturous object of your thoughts and meditations and love and affections and desires? "Arise and depart, this is not your rest." Such is the prophet's striking description of your present position and of your transitory condition here.

CHAPTER II.

THE EARTH NOT THE HOME IN WHICH WE ARE TO LIVE FOR EVER—(*continued.*)

THE home in which you are now spending life is not to be your dwelling-place for ever. Whether you are at present young or old; whether you are rich or poor; whether you are in the palace, with the glittering crown upon your brow, sparkling in your diamonds, and moving in the high places of the earth—or in the lordly hall, exhibiting in your dignity an empty pride, or the meekness of a heavenly wisdom, and patience, and love—or in the cottage, with its hard battle for life and its many trials;—whatever your present home may be, ye are still upon the earth, and, consequently, ye are but pilgrims and strangers here, mere travellers through time; you will not become stationary till you enter yon home that is prepared for you who are the people of God in heaven, and which you will never leave after entering it, whilst the endless cycles of a joyful eternity are rolling over you.

You may now be living in a home of love, upon which the God of your salvation is lifting the light of His countenance, and is showering down upon you, with the widely-opened hand of His beneficence, every temporal blessing, and the whole rich legacies of the covenant of His grace; your life, in your present home, may be encircled and embalmed with an atmosphere of affection; your present Eden-dwelling may be embowered and imparadised by the halo of heaven's own sweet calm;—but still your present home is not the place where you are to take up your habitation for ever; you must, ere long, leave it. The sentence has come out against you individually from Him who is upon the throne, all whose words are true, who ever lives to execute His judgments and to fulfil His threatenings—"Dust thou art, and unto dust shalt thou return." You may have dreamed away, as if in a paradise of flowers, many joyous years in that home over which the sun of an unclouded comfort has hitherto been shining. You may have lived in it for years, with the gladdening stream of God's love, like a river of pure delight, flowing noiselessly through your soul. It may have been to you a Bethel upon earth, the house of God, the gate of heaven: *there*, with its loved and loving inmates, you may have walked together in peace and in the covenant of your God: *there* you may have grown up, with the sunshine of youth upon *your path*, budding into womanhood like the opening, expanding rose, with its leaves all shining in the dew of the morning, or developing into manhood, like the hardy and durable oak, flinging its branches all around, as if making the proclamation that it is the monarch of the wood; so you may have grown up in stature, in knowledge, and in favour with God and with man: *there* God by His Spirit may have been for years carrying on the work of grace in your soul, giving you a meetness to become partakers of the inheritance of the saints in light: *there* you may have become a blushing bride, given away in it by your father, whilst his soul was tumultuated with very commingled emotions in giving you away to the partner of your choice; or, as a bridegroom, you may have entered that home after your return from your marriage jaunt, with the beloved and lovely partner of your affections on your arm, and there felt in her sweet and gentle companionship that a new sun had risen in the firmament of your family experience, and which sun, in the glowing of a warm, and pure, and loving heart, has been shining upon you without a cloud for years: *there* you may have lived the threescore years and ten allotted to man upon the earth;—but long as you have been the inmate of that bower of comparative happiness, you are not to remain in it for ever—you are not to be an eternal *fixture there.*

That home is to you, after all, but an inn; it affords you accommodation merely for a night. The morning of eternity is about to dawn, and ye will then rise up and resume your journey. The trouble has, perchance, already received its commission from God that is to remove you from it. Your present home will soon be inhabited by another tenant; your garden will be kept and dressed by other hands; the silence of a sad and dreary desolation will soon, by your death, be spread over your present happy home; the clock will tick in its loneliness there, but not for you, for you will not be present to hear it; ye will be away, and carried aside from the living, fast asleep in your dreamless slumber, lying in your grave—that silent corner of a living world—motionless, pulseless, and still, with the snowy wreath of the winding-sheet folded carefully by the hand of friendship, and encircling your frozen body.

The summer broods over the earth, with its genial and reviving warmth, and with its sunshine of life; then the flowers spring up in their beauty; the birds sing; the song of their minstrelsy is heard resounding from every wood and from every grove. But the winter arrives in its chariot of clouds and of darkness, mantled in its snow, and surrounded with its body-guard of howling winds and pelting rains; the sun, as if alienated and unfriendly, looks shy and cold upon us, just peeping above the edge of the southern horizon for a little, and then retiring, like a cold friend, paying a cold and formal visit; the song of the birds in the grove is no longer heard; the foliage withers, falls to the earth, and is drifted into wreaths of rustling, restless leaves. The dreary desolation of winter thus succeeds to the life, and warmth, and songs, and loveliness of summer; so will it be with you ere long. The summer of life is now passing over you, with its sunshine and its flowers, and its singing of birds; the light of a bright vernal sky is illuminating your path; and your young unwrinkled brow is encircled by a wreath of roses that are blooming and smiling as sweetly as if they were destined to cluster there for ever and never to fade. But, oh! your winter is coming. I hear its approaching footsteps in the howl of the wind, in the pattering of the sleet and rain upon the windows. The snows, the drifted snows of death, will soon be heaped upon your grave, whilst you, like a withered faded flower, are lying there with all the loveliness of your youth and beauty faded and gone.

The morning dawns with its brightening light, as if gleaming out upon us again and again, in answer to the command which God once issued over a dark and benighted universe, "Let there be light, and there was light." But the day soon passes, the sun, curtained with the western clouds hanging in their crimson drapery around his bed, goes to sleep, retires from our view, and then the darkness of night again pavilions us. So will it be with you. The sun of your existence has risen upon the earth, and is shining in the sky of your present life; but it is not to shine there for ever; soon the silent night of death will be around you; soon your soul will be a sun upraised into the firmament of glory that stretches in its nightless brightness above and around heaven, there to shine through eternity. "The voice said, Cry. And he said, What shall I cry? All flesh is grass, and all the goodliness thereof is as the flower of the field. The grass withereth, the flower fadeth: because the Spirit of the Lord bloweth upon it: surely the people is grass. The grass withereth, the flower fadeth: but the word of our God shall stand for ever." "Like as a father pitieth his children, so the Lord pitieth them that fear him. For he knoweth our frame; he remembereth that we are dust. As for man, his days are as grass; as a flower of the field, so he flourisheth: for the wind passeth over it, and it is gone; and the place thereof shall know it no more." "Go to now, ye that say, To-day or to-morrow we will go into such a city, and continue there a year, and buy and sell, and get gain: whereas ye know not what shall be on the morrow: for what is your life? It is even a vapour, that appeareth for a little time, and then vanisheth away."

This, my readers, is your fleeting and transitory position in the world. You are meteors in the firmament of life, gleaming along a somewhat dark and cloudy sky, and soon from the gaze and weeping eyes of the dear ones you will leave behind you in your home, you will disappear *amid the* gathering and deepening darkness of the night of death. You are but pilgrims and strangers here, as all your fathers were. You are vessels built in the dockyard of the great spirit-land, launched by God himself upon the sea of life, richly laden and freighted with the treasures of immortality; the sheeted sea around you is radiant with the gleam and the sunshine of your immortal hopes; you are gliding on with outstretched sail along the bosom of the great deep, and lo! you see before you, in its bright and glassy calm, the ocean of glory that is flowing round about the throne of God; and soon you will leave, not the British Channel to enter the broad Atlantic, but the sea of life here and cross over into the ocean of glory yonder, and there you will sail for ever in an ocean of beatitude that is bounded by no shore. You are pilgrims upon life's rugged, and often desolate and dreary path; your journey, however, will soon be ended, and then, during a long, joyous, and blissful eternity, you will enter upon the rest that remains for the people of God.

Man is now seen going to his long home, and the mourners are going about the streets. The newly upturned earth of many a lonely grave is surrounded by sorrowful funeral attendants. The living in their robes of mourning are seen standing around the dead, consigning with tears the departed to their narrow bed, where they are to sleep till awakened by the blast of the archangel's trumpet. The day of the Lord, however, will come. The last funeral party will meet at the burial-place, it may be in the beautiful and sequestered church-yard of ——. The mourners will be around the opened grave; they will take the cords, will slowly, solemnly, and sadly, let down the coffin with its sleeping inmate to its appointed place of rest; the funeral attendants will lift their hats, both in the act of bidding a respectful farewell to the dead, and also of lifting their souls in secret prayer to Him with whom is the fountain of life; the church-officer will take his spade, and begin to shovel in the loose excavated earth, with the object of burying the dead out of the sight of the living. Stop, sexton! You need not go on with your work. Look up! What light is yon that has just now burst into view, and that is gleaming over us in the sky, above the brightness of the sun, like an ocean of glory opening its great white bosom, and pouring forth its tremendous floods of living, crystal waters, or like a continent of drifting snow, all in sparkling, glittering, luminous motion, and is pouring itself down from heaven, and is speeding towards the earth with the rapidity of the lightning's flash, that gleams out of one part under heaven and shines unto the other in the twinkling of an eye? That is no passing meteor; it is no vapouring, careering comet, that is sailing over the earth's orbit in its journey through the great pavilion of space; it is no mere angelic messenger, such as threw the splendour of his presence over the midnight plains of Bethlehem, when the Son of the Highest became a child born and a son given. It is Christ himself, the Sun of Righteousness, bursting forth upon the gaze of a startled world in His own glory, in the glory of the Father, and in the glory of all His holy angels, coming to call the long-forgotten dead from their long, silent, and dreamless sleep, and to change the living. What rumbling, half-suppressed, rolling sound is that which is falling upon the ears of these sorrowful mourners who are encircling that opened grave, at the bottom of which the yet uncovered coffin is lying? Is it the sobbings of these mourners, who are in tears as they look down upon the dear one lying cold beneath their feet. No! for they are looking up, and their faces are all upturned in wonder, in amazement, and with something like the blanched looks and the chokings of terror, towards the descending burst of melodious voices that they hear sounding above them in the sky, as if many thousand-tongued choirs of earth had suddenly met as one in the firmament, and had begun to pour forth their united voices in an anthem of sweetest praise to that God who sitteth in awful majesty above. Oh! it is the heavenly anthem sung by the whole collected hosts of angels, the outbursting roll of praise from the descending myriads of the just made perfect, who are pouring forth their heavenly and holy hallelujahs to Jesus; proclaiming in exulting triumph over this world of graves, "Salvation to him that sitteth upon the throne, and unto the Lamb that was slain."

The reign of temporal death is over! The jubilee of the grave has dawned! The prisoners of the tomb are now for ever free! Lo! the Lord Jesus speaks from the throne! It is the same voice that issued the command on the morning of creation over a dead and benighted universe, "Let there be light, and there was light." It is the same voice that was heard at the tomb of Lazarus, saying, "Lazarus, come forth." That voice is now calling to the nations, and kindreds, and peoples, and tongues who are lying in the grave, "Arise, ye dead, and come to judgment." What a change over the whole surface of the earth and throughout its oceans and seas will that call make! In a moment millions of millions and millions more of the long-forgotten dead will be on their feet and mingling with the living world again. The great white throne is the centre around which they assemble and gather in prodigious numbers from the four winds of heaven. Oh, with what a thrill of joy do the congregated children of God listen to Christ's voice saying to them, whilst pointing upwards with the finger of His love into the opening, glorious heaven, already prepared and made ready for their admission, "Come, ye blessed of my Father, inherit the kingdom prepared for you before the foundation of the world!" The *moment* these words fall upon the ears of the people of God, they will not only look up, but begin to rise upwards to the place of their eternal rest, the Lord Jesus leaving the throne and leading the way. Over the waving assemblages rising upwards towards heaven, a voice will be heard saying, Lift up your heads, O ye gates, even lift them up, ye everlasting doors, that God's great family may come in. They enter—they are home for ever!

CHAPTER III.

HEAVEN AS A WORLD OF LIFE IS TOO LITTLE REALISED.

PERHAPS the grandest panorama which the eye of man can survey is the visible heavens, on a calm, clear, frosty night, all in a gleam, and glittering with the outbursting brilliancy of thousands of stars. It was the view of this scene that led the Psalmist to burst forth in these words of wonder and of adoration, "When I consider thy heavens, the work of thy fingers, the moon and the stars, which thou hast ordained; what is man, that thou art mindful of him? and the son of man, that thou visitest him?"

No one can look, on such an occasion, upon these numberless orbs, shining in their quiet and far-off spheres, without feeling the question spontaneously rising in his mind—Are these stars inhabited like our earth? Is there a life overspreading them all, such as we see around us here? Is there the hum of a busy and active population rising from the surface of each? The Scriptures are silent upon this subject, and thus all the knowledge about it which philosophers have yet been able to give us is a mere *conjecture,* that in each of the orbs composing our solar system, and in each of the fixed stars, "life" *may* have its development, and the great God, who is reigning over all, *may* have His intelligent worshippers.

The Scriptures speak to us about only three worlds in God's great universe that are peopled, and in which living intelligences are spending that life which God has conferred upon them—*earth, hell, heaven.* We know from experience and observation about the life that man is now spending upon the earth. We know from the Scriptures, and through the gloomy foreshadowings of an awakened conscience, *something* of the life which fallen angels, and the already lost members of the human family, are spending in hell. We know from the same lively oracles of God, and through those blessed religious experiences which Christians enjoy upon earth—and which are just so many earnests and foretastes of heaven—what the life is which the already glorified are now spending with their God and Saviour on high.

There is such a thing as "Life in Heaven" as well as life upon earth, for heaven is peopled, and the life its inhabitants are spending is often referred to in the Bible. But how little is this realised by the generality of Christians! Strange this should be in the experience of those who have the Scriptures in their hands!

Look at this strange phenomenon through the following supposition: Suppose we had the same evidence that one of the fixed stars is inhabited that we have that heaven is,—that not one, but many well-authenticated communications had come down from those living in it to the inhabitants of earth, at sundry times and in divers manners,—that the sovereign who presides over it had often descended, appeared to men upon earth, and spoken to them audibly in words which they perfectly understood,—that the son of that sovereign had left his father's palace for a number of years, and with a bosom all in a glow of unquenchable love to the whole members of the human family, and on a mission of the highest importance to us, had descended into this world, had lit upon its surface, had mingled freely with us in all the amenities and familiar associations of life, had frequently and unreservedly talked to us about yonder star he had left, about its *inhabitants*, their *dignity*, their *number*, their *employments*, their *intercourse*,—that not one, but many of its inhabitants had come out from their compeers, and down into this world, to execute at their sovereign's behest their appointed messages, had appeared to us face to face, had spoken freely about the orb they had left, and of the interest which their fellows feel in us,—that we had seen one generation of the human family after another, our dear friends at their death, leaving us with the full confidence, based upon the most undoubted evidence, that they were to ascend and find a home for eternity in yon beautiful star, whose inhabitants are never sick, and never die:—how vivid in this case would our view be of our future and eternal habitation, and of the life which those are spending who are there before us!

All this has actually taken place in reference to heaven. How is it, then, that our views about *it* are so dim, and shadowy, and obscure? This arises, partly at least, from the *fact* that things that are seen impress us far more forcibly than things do which are not seen, and partly from a weakness of faith—a want of that spiritual power of mind by which we realise the *unseen* and the *eternal.*

It will aid our realisations of heaven, if we accustom ourselves to look up into it, not merely through the express announcements made to us about it in the Bible, but also through the medium of what is *seen;* for God's lower and material creation is *probably* just the counterpart to a great extent of His higher and heavenly one. Do we look upon the sun by day, shining forth upon our view from his pavilion of light? In that sun we see mirrored the Great Father of Lights making Himself visible to the inhabitants of heaven, who covers Himself with light as with a garment, who dwells amid the light that is inaccessible and full of glory; and Christ's visible glory is also seen imaged there, who is the Sun of Righteousness, the Light of heaven, and the Glory of eternity. Look we upon the stars in the midnight sky, gleaming forth upon our view in their peaceful, far-off spheres? In their quiet, silvery twinkling, great in number, high in station, and pure to the eye as the sparkling diamond,—in these bright orbs, we see the visible exemplification of angels, the morning stars of heaven, and of glorified saints, who shine so high and so resplendently *before, above*, and *round about* the throne of God, like the brightness of the firmament, and as the stars for ever and ever. Do we look upon God's green earth, that is now our dwelling-place and scene of preparation for an oncoming eternity, so densely populated, and so full of life, business, and activity? —in this we see heaven mirrored, as the sky and surrounding scenery are reflected in a pure lake, as your image is in the glass that stands in your room—for heaven is a world as well as this; it has its life, its dense population, its sky above them, and its immortal inhabitants living together in high and holy intercourse. Do we survey a congregation of God's worshipping people met in their house of prayer for God's public worship and praise?—*there* we see heaven made visible, whose holy worshippers are joining in the high praises of eternity. Do we look upon a Christian home, with its inmates united in a common brotherhood, dwelling together in love, and spending life in its nearest, dearest, and holiest relationships?—*there* we see heaven mirrored, and the family of the great God above portrayed, who now inhabit the building of God, the house not made with hands, eternal in the heavens. Do we look upon the light overshadowing us by day?—in *that* overflowing ocean of light we see mirrored the unending day and the light of a blessed eternity that is above and around and so peacefully overflowing the world of glory on high.

We have need of such aid as this to enable us to realise the unseen, for verily our views about heaven are dim and obscure. Heaven is out of sight, and too much out of mind, and thus, alas! even among Christians, it is too seldom the subject of conversation in their social circles. There are many ministers, and there are many even pious Christians, who seem to shrink from speaking or writing about heaven, about its inhabitants, and about the life they are spending before the God of their salvation on high. Heaven, in the view of these individuals apparently, for they scarcely ever speak about it, is a world too sacred to be spoken about; and the portion of the already-glorified is a something too high, too mysterious, too transcendently grand, for them even to attempt to describe. Thus, whilst talking freely to each other about the politics, the trade, the affairs of earth; the things of heaven—its inhabitants, their glory, their bliss—are but seldom, if they are ever, alluded to at all.

In proof of this, I ask you, whom I now address through these pages, to notice your conversation with your friends whilst sitting with them in your homes, or whilst walking with them by the way, and you will find that, in the midst of the almost infinite variety of subjects that in succession become the themes of your observation, *heaven* and the *glorious inhabitants* who dwell in its courts are scarcely ever referred to; or if heaven is looked into for a passing moment, it is with a gloom upon the soul, like what a person experiences when entering a dark cave—the desire is to get away from the scene as soon as possible. It is difficult to account for this;—people don't generally recoil from speaking about their home when at a distance from it;—whether it arises from a state in us of utter worldly-mindedness, or from inability, through the weakness of faith, to apprehend and realise the things of God, of eternity, of heaven. The Scriptures seem to attribute this somewhat strange phenomenon to the latter cause: "But the natural man receiveth not the things of the Spirit of God: for they are foolishness unto him: neither can he know them, because they are spiritually discerned."

We believe, indeed, in the existence of a heaven of glory above, which is to be our eternal home, where God has established His throne, a throne of glory that is high and lifted up, and where the reflections of His manifested presence are spreading over it and through it the light and the splendour of a never-ending day. We believe that Jesus is there, enthroned at the right hand of the Majesty on high, in honour and glory, the brightness of the Father's glory, and the express image of His person. We believe that the Holy Spirit is now filling heaven with the light of His ineffable presence, and with the glow of His celestial love. We believe that troops of angels in their battalions of life, majesty, and glory, are even at this very moment crowding the streets of the heavenly Jerusalem, and are throwing the halo of their bright appearance upwards upon the blue concave that arches the fair heavens, like the calm sea becoming bright when the clear morning sun shines forth from the east upon it. We believe that there are now in heaven an innumerable company of the saved from earth, even a multitude of the human family which no man can number, collected into its happy courts, out of every nation, and kindred, and people, and tongue. We believe that all the redeemed who are now in heaven have entered upon a portion of inexpressible glory, of unutterable joy, of unending felicity in God's presence, where there is fulness of joy, and at His right hand, where there are pleasures for evermore. We believe that some who are now in heaven were the inmates of our home whilst they yet remained in this world below, worshipped God with us in the same sanctuary, kneeled with us at our family altar, and conversed with us once about the things they now see and enjoy.

We thus implicitly *believe* in the *existence* of a *heaven* of glory above us, with its peace, and its calm, and its holy joys, and its Sabbath that never ends, and its white-robed assemblies, who are all life and alacrity in the missions, and worship, and praise of God. But *with* this belief, how *dim* does heaven appear to us! How *dead*, how *cold*, how *empty*, how *dull*, does it come out to our upward gaze—to the eye of our faith! How greatly do we come short of a living faith's full realisation of it! How is this? How are our views of heaven, in which some of our dear friends now dwell, dimmer than our views of a foreign land are, which we have never seen, and to which some of our friends may have emigrated, and in which they are now dwelling, separated from us by the deep, blue sea? You perhaps have friends in a distant land. They parted from you, and went to the home where they now dwell. You have not forgotten them any more than they have forgotten you; your fond recollections of them still cluster and hang upon the walls of the chamber of your memory. You often think about them, you often speak about them, and delight to recollect them, and to view them as still living, in your conversation with those around you. You have friends also in heaven, the better country, that is, the heavenly. Are they, I ask, as vividly the objects of your contemplation as your friends in a foreign land are? I know your answer will be, they are not; you fail, often for days and for weeks, to realise their existence at all, or the existence of yonder heaven, in which they have their abiding home. Why should this be? Your departed friends, who have fallen asleep in Jesus, are not out of existence. The swallow does not go out of existence when, at the approach of winter, it emigrates from our cold and northern clime to seek a warmer home in the sunny south. The ship does not cease to be, when, with outspread sails, it leaves the harbour, and glides off from us, and beyond the reach of our eye, upon the bosom of the ocean, that it may enter the haven of security and repose on the other side. The eagle does not lose its existence by rising upwards from the valley, ascending with outspread wings to the highest cliff of the lofty mountain. Neither do God's children lose *their* existence at death. *Then* their souls, still *living*, rise from earth, and enter into a living heaven.

The sacred writers never lose sight of this great truth, however much we may do so. They follow, in their believing and realising contemplations, the upward flight of God's children to heaven, and speak frequently to us about *where* they are, and about *what* they are doing, and about the *life* they are spending yonder. The whole of God's children who have left this world, who have passed through the valley of the shadow of death, are still in life. They are living in heaven. "For we know that if our earthly house of this tabernacle were dissolved, we have a building of God, an house not made with hands, eternal in the heavens." "And when he had opened the fifth seal, I saw under the altar the souls of them that were slain for the word of God, and for the testimony which they held: and they cried with a loud voice, saying, How long, O Lord, holy and true, dost thou not judge and avenge our blood on them that dwell on the earth? And white robes were given unto every one of them; and it was said unto them, that they should rest yet for a little season, until their fellow-servants also and their brethren, that should be killed as they were, should be fulfilled." "After this I beheld, and, lo, a great multitude, which no man could number, of all nations, and kindreds, and people, and tongues, stood before the throne, and before the Lamb, clothed with white robes, and palms in their hands; and cried with a loud voice, saying, Salvation to our God which sitteth upon the throne, and unto the Lamb."

TWO EFFECTS WILL FOLLOW THIS HABITUAL REALISATION OF HEAVEN AS A WORLD OF LIFE AND OF REWARD.

1. *Comfort to you who are the children of God.*

Is the world to you dark and dreary? There is *an eternity* of light awaiting you in heaven. Is life to you a scene of sorrow? An immortality of joy is to be yours above. Are you sick *here?* Endless health awaits you *yonder.* Are you in your death-chamber, with your heart and flesh fainting and failing? Be not cast down. You are crossing the Jordan in company with Jesus, the Ark of the Covenant. The promised land is opening to your view. You are just about to emerge from the floods to enter upon the existence of heaven, and there eternal life will be yours. Are you in the chamber where a dear friend is dying, with the sad anticipation of the parting near? Friends, dear, fondly and deeply beloved, are living in heaven, and, with the gushing joys of an intense and ecstatic welcome, are about to receive your dying friend, and you, when you follow, up into a heaven of love, to join their gladdened throngs. Cheer up, child of God! The night is far spent, the day is at hand. Soon the voice of a Father's invitation will fall, like good news from a far country, upon thine ear, whilst stretched upon a dying pillow: "Well done, good and faithful servant, enter thou into the joy of thy Lord." "I have a desire to depart, and to be with Christ, which is far better."

2. *Such a view of heaven will be a powerful motive for present exertion in the ways of the Lord.*

In life we feel that the view of what we are to secure in the future operates as a powerful motive to present exertion. The student pores over his books, gathers the thoughts of others into the storehouse of his own mind, diligently and anxiously prepares himself for the position of life he wishes to obtain ;—the merchant, whose trade is carried on with foreign lands, embarks fearlessly upon the stormy ocean, faces the dangers of the deep, absents himself from his home and from his family for months and for years—his eye all the while being directed to that peaceful. retirement in the evening of life which his business successfully prosecuted will one day secure to him and to his family ;—the husbandman, in the midst of the snows and the rains and the blustering winds of winter, ploughs his fields and prepares his seed, which he sows in the spring, having all the while the luxuriant harvest of autumn in his view ;—the soldier, in the midst of the toils and dangers and the horrors of war, exposes himself by night and by day to a bloody, and it may be to an instantaneous death, stimulated by the view of that crown of honour and of applause, which loyalty to his sovereign and devotion to his country's cause will one day entwine around his brow ;—the mariner, whilst afloat upon the ocean, spreads the sail, guides the helm, keeps his eye upon the compass, that he may thus be guided in the right course—all this he does with the object of reaching the haven which is still at a great distance from him ;—the competitor in the arena at the Olympic games kept his eye upon the crown placed in his view at the end of the race-course, and, gazing upon the prize, earnestly put forth his utmost exertion to gain it.

The same is true of the children of God who are still in the world: it is the view of the glory that is yet to be revealed—the crown, the haven, the reward—that stimulates us to go on perseveringly with our works of faith and labours of love; it is the view, by faith, of the heavens expanding and stretching above us and around us, in all their magnificence, and grandeur, and glory, and bliss, that becomes, through the influence of a holy hope, animated by a realising faith, a powerful, nay, something like an irresistible motive, leading us to "lay aside every weight, and the sin which doth most easily beset us, and to run with patience the race that is set before us, looking unto Jesus, the author and finisher of our faith; who, for the joy that was set before him, endured the cross, despising the shame, and is set down at the right hand of the throne of God."

CHAPTER IV.

HEAVEN THE ETERNAL HOME OF THE CHILDREN OF GOD—FAITH'S GLIMPSE INTO IT.

AN earthly home is not always within the view of the members of the family who belong to it: distance may remove it beyond the reach of their eye: the want of sight may prevent them from seeing it even while it is near. Heaven is to be, to us who are the children of God, our eternal home; but at present it is not the object of sight to us. Whether this arises from distance or the want of the bodily faculty of seeing it, whatever be the cause, heaven is as much out of our view as if it were at present not in existence at all.

Heaven, however, *does* exist, and, moreover, it has been at different times unveiled, and has become the object of sight to some of the children of God, even whilst they were yet dwelling upon the earth; and in the inspired descriptions recorded in the Bible, they tell us what they saw when to their uplifted and wondering eye they beheld the heavens open, and its crowding assemblies in their robes of white flitting to and fro through its courts of glory. "I saw the Lord sitting on his throne," says the prophet Micaiah, "and all the host of heaven standing by him on his right hand and on his left." Isaiah thus describes what he saw, when, in the visions of the Almighty, he looked up into the opened heavens and beheld its great Sovereign upon the throne of His glory: "In the year that king Uzziah died I saw also the Lord sitting upon a throne, high and lifted up, and his train filled the temple." The heavens are opened to the view of Stephen, for his support and comfort at the hour of his cruel martyrdom, and thus is described what he then beheld: "But he, being full of the Holy Ghost, looked up stedfastly into heaven, and saw the glory of God, and Jesus standing on the right hand of God, and said, Behold, I see the heavens opened, and the Son of man standing on the right hand of God." The apostle John, above all who ever lived upon earth, is favoured with the heavens again and again opened to the view of his bodily eye, and thus he speaks of what he saw: "After this I looked, and, behold, a door was opened in heaven: and the first voice which I heard was as it were of a trumpet talking with me; which said, Come up hither, and I will shew thee things which must be hereafter. And immediately I was in the Spirit: and, behold, a throne was set in heaven, and one sat on the throne. And he that sat was to look upon like a jasper and a sardine stone: and there was a rainbow round about the throne, in sight like unto an emerald. And round about the throne were four and twenty seats: and upon the seats I saw four and twenty elders sitting, clothed in white raiment; and they had on their heads crowns of gold." "And I beheld, and I heard the voice of many angels round about the throne, and the beasts, and the elders: and the number of them was ten thousand times ten thousand, and thousands of thousands; saying with a loud voice, Worthy is the Lamb that was slain to receive power, and riches, and wisdom, and strength, and honour, and glory, and blessing." "After this I beheld, and, lo, a great multitude, which no man could number, of all nations, and kindreds, and people, and tongues, stood before the throne, and before the Lamb, clothed with white robes, and palms in their hands; and cried with a loud voice, saying, Salvation to our God which sitteth upon the throne, and unto the Lamb."

Heaven does not appear to our view as it did to the bodily eyes of these children of God, whose descriptions of it I have thus given. Heaven is to us what the holy of holies was to the Israelites of old—curtained off by a veil of invisibility and hidden from us. The Israelites saw not, with the bodily eye, into the holy of holies; they had merely particular descriptions of it in the Scriptures which were in their hands; these they could read, and, through their descriptions, they could *in faith* look in upon that awfully solemn and sacred chamber where God in the cloud appeared upon the mercy-seat, and shone forth from between the cherubim. This is our position in reference to heaven. We see it not with the bodily eye, but we have particular and inspired descriptions of it given us in the Bible by those who have looked into it, and we can now use these descriptions as so many telescopes through which we can look up and in upon the otherwise hidden heavens, and behold in all its life and magnificence the world of glory above.

These inspired descriptions of heaven thus do for us what a treatise on geography does for us in behalf of a country we never saw; what a memoir does for us in behalf of an individual we never met; what the telescope does to the astronomer in reference to a portion of the material universe. There are orbs existing in the material universe so far distant from us in space that they are entirely hidden from the view of our bodily eye; stars are in existence which the unaided eye of man never reached in their far-off stations in space, and which we could never have known did exist had the telescope not been invented: the telescope, however, pierces by its penetrating glance the hidden recesses of space, lifts the veil that conceals them from our view, and lays open to our observation not single stars merely, but glittering firmaments grouped into their respective family clusters, dimly but plainly shining like so many islands of light in the great, encircling ocean of space.

Heaven, like the remote star, is hidden from our view; but we have in the Scriptures a divine telescope through whose revelations we can look up and in upon that holy place; and all that is now, on our part, needed to see into it as our eternal home is the eye of faith, brought into relation with these Scriptures, that speak to us about it and about its living assemblies. "Faith is the substance of things hoped for, the evidence of things not seen." Faith is the eye that looks through the glass of God's Word, and up through the windows of heaven, and beholds its living assemblies. Yes, yonder sanctuary that is above us, and which, in the view of the unbeliever, is a mere name, a great idea, or at most a vast and undefined region, comes forth into the view of the believer's eye a great world of life, peopled with innumerable inhabitants, met together for eternity before the throne of God, and dwelling together in all the sweet and social intercourse of love and of home.

Reader! look up and view with me yonder bright home of love which God has prepared for His children beyond death and the grave. The representation of it as a home is by far the most delightful description of it which the sacred writers give us in the Scriptures,—a home into which many of the children of God are entering when they go up into it from their beds of death. And what a comforting thought it is to those entering that they will never require to leave it permanently, or to bid those who are there a final adieu! The time never will come, throughout the annals of an oncoming eternity, when the family of God will require to flit, and leave that refuge for some other habitation. "For we know, that, if our earthly house of this tabernacle were dissolved, we have a building of God, an house not made with hands, eternal in the heavens." Death will never again part those who meet in that house, for it is a world of life: there is in its happy courts no more death, neither sorrow nor crying, neither is there any more pain, for the former things are passed away.

Different are the families of the children of God in their homes of change upon earth. The sportiveness of children in their parents' home, gambolling away in each other's company the morning of life, is soon exchanged for the silence and the gloom that brood over the graves of that whole household. The happiest family upon earth, in their home of love, is soon startled by the knock at their door of the king of terrors, and at the sound of the voice which summons them successively away. It is not so in heaven's high and happy home. When the children of God meet in yonder abode of bliss, they meet to part no more.

I now wish the reader to look up with me, and in upon that eternal home of life and of love, whilst I endeavour to give a short description of the high and happy inmates now assembled there, and who will be there through eternity.

THE UNCREATED INMATES OF HEAVEN.

God our Father is there. The first petition in the Lord's Prayer teaches us this great truth: "Our Father in heaven." Again, Jesus says, "Take heed that ye despise not one of these little ones: for I say unto you, That in heaven their angels do always behold the face of my Father which is in heaven." God is everywhere present throughout His great universe; for the heavens, even the heaven of heavens, cannot contain Him: but in a peculiar manner He vouchsafes His presence and the rich manifestations of His glory and love to those who are there. This is the comforting and soul-refreshing view of God which He gives us of Himself in the gospel of His grace. God appears in heaven as a father in the midst of his family. The inmates see God, not merely in the Person of Christ; they see God himself; they possess the beatific vision—the vision that makes happy; they see God upon the throne in all His glory, and beauty, and love, are satisfied with His likeness, and rejoice in His smile,—that smile which spreads the light of an eternal day over all who are in glory. "Blessed are the pure in heart, for they shall see God." "And they shall see his face, and his name shall be in their foreheads." God is a sovereign upon the throne, but He is also a Father—the Father of mercies and the God of all comfort, manifesting His presence to all the members of His great family who are living with Him on high. With the smile of a father upon His countenance, and with the love of a father glowing in His bosom, He is holding high and blissful communion not merely with Jesus, the Son of His love, and with the Holy Spirit,—He is also condescending, in all the love, and tenderness, and sympathy of a father in the midst of His children, to hold sweet and endearing intercourse with the whole created inmates of heaven. He rests in His love towards them, He rejoices in their joy, He listens to their praise, He walks with them, and holds high and ineffable converse with them. He is their sun and shield; they are in His presence, spending a glad eternity beneath the overshadowings of His glory, and encircled with the joys of His own glad heaven. "The sun shall be no more thy light by day; neither for brightness shall the moon give light unto thee: but the Lord shall be unto thee an everlasting light, and thy God thy glory. Thy sun shall no more go down; neither shall thy moon withdraw itself: for the Lord shall be thine everlasting light, and the days of thy mourning shall be ended. Thy people also shall be all righteous: they shall inherit the land for ever, the branch of my planting, the work of my hands, that I may be glorified."

The Holy Spirit is manifesting His blessed presence to all who are in yonder glorious home. With our present limited faculties, it is impossible that we can now form a clear and definite conception of the personality and distinct individuality either of the First or of the Third Person of the adorable Godhead. It is easy to form a definite conception of the personality of Christ, for He has our nature, and now appears in heaven wearing the human form. The Holy Spirit, however, has a distinct personality, though we cannot describe in what it consists, or even conceive what it is; and, as one of the three Persons of the Godhead, the Holy Spirit is now appearing with the Father and the Son to all who are in heaven. He is a Person who has life in Himself and who gives life to others—making believers the new creation of God in Christ Jesus; who forms, in His Divine mind, the large and comprehensive plan of God's mercy to man in the work of human redemption, and who writes, or rather dictates, the Book of Life which reveals it; who loves, who sorrows, who is vexed, who is grieved, who sympathises with the sorrowing, who comforts the downcast and broken in spirit. The Holy Spirit does this to us and feels thus with us, whilst all the time He remains invisible to our bodily eye. But He is acting differently to those who are in heaven. He appears to them in His glory. He manifests Himself in His life and love to their view.

The Lord Jesus is now in heaven upon the throne with God, and is there appearing in His glory to all its happy inmates. The heavens have received Him until the final restitution of all things. "Seeing then that we have a great high priest, that is passed into the heavens, Jesus the Son of God, let us hold fast our profession." "Him hath God exalted with his right hand to be a Prince and a Saviour, for to give repentance to Israel, and forgiveness of sins." It is only when looking up with the eye of faith that we can say with the apostle, "But we see Jesus, who was made a little lower than the angels for the suffering of death, crowned with glory and honour; that he by the grace of God should taste death for every man." Those who are in heaven see Jesus eye to eye without a veil between,—they see Him as He is,—they behold Him now at the right hand of the throne of God, the brightness of the Father's glory, and the express image of His person. They see Him and hear Him as He makes intercession with the Father in behalf of His Church and people; they see Him in His love, as He presents the prayers of all saints to Him who is upon the throne. As He receives His people to Himself, so He presents them to the Father, and rejoices over them in the fulfilment of this prayer: "Father, I will that they also, whom thou hast given me, be with me where I am; that they may behold my glory, which thou hast given me: for thou lovedst me before the foundation of the world."

How glorious does Jesus now appear to the assemblies above, compared with what He did once to the inhabitants of this world! Here, Christ is seen with saddened countenance and sorrowful brow, a man of sorrows, and acquainted with grief. Yonder, He beams forth upon heaven's admiring assemblies, shining in all the glories of the Godhead. Here, His face was so marred more than any man, and His form than the sons of men; in the garden of Gethsemane it was beclouded with sweat and blood. Yonder, Christ's face is fairer than the children of men; His countenance is like the sun shining in his strength. Here, Christ's eyes were seen often dim with sorrow, red with weeping, and on the cross closing in death. Yonder, His eyes are as a flame of fire, searching Jerusalem as with lighted candles. Here, His head in cruel mockery was encircled with a crown of thorns; the prickles were forced by the pitiless soldiers into His sacred brow; the blood, in a trickling stream, flowed from the opened wounds. Yonder, Christ is diademed with a crown of glory that fadeth not away; He hath upon His head many crowns, and is acknowledged by all who are in heaven as their King and Lord. Here, He was arrayed with the purple robe; the reed of insult was put into His hand; and the mocking Jews, in derision, bowed to Him the knee. Yonder, Christ is arrayed with the robe of uncreated glory; He covers Himself with light, as with a garment; the sceptre of universal empire is in His hand, and all the hosts of heaven are bowing before Him. Here, He was surrounded by many who hated Him without a cause, and who lifted vociferously the cry, "Away with him, away with him; crucify him, crucify him." Yonder, Christ is encircled alone by those who love Him, and who will through all eternity hymn forth His praises in heaven. Here, Christ was lifted upon the cross a spectacle of woe to angels and to men. Yonder, He is exalted upon the throne, and numbers without number are raising before Him this hallelujah acclaim, "Salvation to him that sitteth upon the throne, and unto the Lamb for ever and ever." Christ will thus appear in His glory to all who are in heaven, and will, with all the intenseness of the holiest love, commune with them freely, and face to face, throughout the endless ages of a glad eternity.

THE CREATED INMATES OF HEAVEN'S HIGH HOME.

There are two distinct orders of created beings who dwell in heaven, and make up God's family there—angels, and the already glorified members of the human family. Angels are there. We know nothing about angels further than what the Bible has made known to us. Our knowledge of their existence, and of what they are, is entirely derived from the Word of God. Whilst contemplating what the Bible reveals to us about these high intelligences, do not overlook the *fact*, that the Bible does not *profess* to give us a history of angels and of God's dealings with them. The Bible is simply an inspired description of what God has done *with* and *for* the human family, in effecting the great work of our redemption. All the allusions the Scriptures make to angels are merely incidental, made on account of their associations and intercourse with man.

Hence, there are many things which we might desire to know about these high intelligences upon which the Bible is entirely silent: the *time* of their creation—how *long* it was before the creation of man; the *order* of their creation—whether created all at once, or successively, after long intervals, like the human race; the *agency* of their *creation*—whether direct, by God's high and immediate behest, as Adam was, or by parental transmission; the *nature* of their *essence*—whether purely spiritual, or matter spiritualised and in possession of high intelligence; the *constitution* of their *persons*—whether made up of pure spirit, such as we believe the Father and the Holy Spirit to be, or of a body and spirit such as Jesus is and man is; the *way* in which they obtain a knowledge of us, and of what is taking place upon earth—whether through the medium of certain senses, like ours, being brought into direct and immediate contact with us, in their missions from heaven to earth, or by a full, and something like a divine intuition, beholding at once the whole expanded and unfolded universe of God laid open to their view, including the very inmost chambers of the soul of man—such an inspection and scrutiny of all existences as we believe the adorable Godhead exercises ; the *manner* in which they convey an account of the knowledge which they have gained about what is taking place upon earth to the created inmates of heaven—whether by a personal return to heaven with the intelligence, or by sending at times the account with other angels whom they meet in their walks through the world, and who are about to rise immediately to heaven, like vessels crossing each other's path, and sending a verbal or written message home ; or whether, by something like the cords of an electric sympathy, stretching betwixt earth and heaven, along which in a moment, in the twinkling of an eye, they can transmit an account to those in glory of anything they may know to be interesting to them, dwelling in the realms of eternal day.

The Scriptures, however, make known to us much incidentally respecting these angels of God : that they were created before the earth was, or man was formed, for when God, on the morning of creation, summoned into existence the heavens and the earth, "the morning stars sang together, and the sons of

God shouted for joy;"—that heaven is their usual habitation and home, where they are made glad by a habitual and uninterrupted view of the face of God: "Take heed that ye despise not one of these little ones: for I say unto you, That in heaven their angels do always behold the face of my Father which is in heaven;"—that they differ in rank—angels, archangels, principalities, powers, cherubim, seraphim;—that their rank in heaven is high—sons of God, morning stars, undying courtiers in the high palace of eternity;—that their form is beautiful and their appearance bright: "And I saw another mighty angel come down from heaven, clothed with a cloud; and a rainbow was upon his head, and his face was as it were the sun, and his feet as pillars of fire;"—that they are immortal, and will thus never die: "Neither can they die any more: for they are equal unto the angels; and are the children of God, being the children of the resurrection;"—that their number is very great: "The chariots of God are twenty thousand, even thousands of angels: the Lord is among them, as in Sinai, in the holy place:" "And I beheld, and I heard the voice of many angels round about the throne, and the beasts, and the elders: and the number of them was ten thousand times ten thousand, and thousands of thousands;"—that they join in the worship of God: "And all the angels stood round about the throne, and about the elders and the four beasts, and fell before the throne on their faces, and worshipped God, saying, Amen: Blessing, and glory, and wisdom, and thanksgiving, and honour, and power, and might, be unto our God for ever and ever: Amen;"—that they hold converse, and are able to communicate intelligence to the members of the human family: "And the angel said unto them, Fear not: for, behold, I bring you good tidings of great joy, which shall be to all people;"—that they feel a deep interest in us: "Likewise, I say unto you, there is joy in the presence of the angels of God over one sinner that repenteth;"—that they are our guardians here during life, and bear us home to heaven at death. In heaven, angels will associate with us for eternity, and will freely communicate to us what they have seen and what they know of the ways and works of God.

There are also in heaven a great number of the human family who are already glorified.

I have already given in another treatise, "Meet for Heaven," what I believe to be the Scriptural view of "a state of glory;" and in connexion with this, what those members of the human family are, and now experience, who have gone up from earth, and have entered upon the "Life in Heaven." I may here add, that the glorified in heaven are just what they were in their religious experiences whilst they were in "a state of grace" upon earth, only they are perfected. They love yonder the same God whom they loved here. They are looking with a heavenly affection to the same Saviour whom they loved and followed whilst upon earth. Their souls are warmed with the glowings of divine love, and their lips are tuned to the praises of God by the same Holy Spirit who was their life, and shed abroad the love of God in their hearts here. They possess the same social nature, the same delight in the communion of the saints, which they had upon earth. They that feared the Lord spake often one to another, the Lord hearkened and heard them, whilst they were upon earth. They are doing the same now that they have met in heaven. Thus you who are the children of God can look up to a social heaven which is to be your eternal home, into which death is to usher you, there to meet and to associate for ever with Father, Son, and Holy Spirit, with angels, and with all the glorified members of the human family.

CHAPTER V.

THE DYING BELIEVER IN HIS SICK CHAMBER ON THE THRESHOLD OF HEAVEN.

THE sick chamber of a dying believer is the gate of heaven. Death to a believer is the opening of the gate of glory by Christ, who has in the hand of His sovereignty the keys of death and of the invisible world; it is thus God's child enters into heaven, his Father's home. I am in the hope that an illustration of this view of being "on the threshold" will help to dispel the gloom which the approaching night of death brings around the bed of dissolution, and shew to the eye of holy hope the morning, dawning around that bed, of a day that is never to end.

What a trying and affecting position you are in, ye children of God, who are now in your chamber of sickness, whose heart and flesh are fainting and failing, and who are looking forward, either in a state of anxiety, or with your soul stayed upon the Lord Jesus, serene and calm, with the anticipation that the hour of your dissolution is near! You have bidden adieu to the world ; your connexion with its life, its business, its activity, is already in a great measure terminated. God has taken you by the hand, has turned aside with you from the world, and is overshadowing you with His covenant and gracious presence in your chamber of affliction. Do not faint when thus rebuked of Him. "He afflicteth not willingly, neither grieveth the children of men." "Whom the Lord loveth he chasteneth, and scourgeth every son whom he receiveth." God does not free you from affliction, but remember when in it He has taken you into your sick chamber, that from it you may rise and enter a heaven of life. Is not the knowledge of this to you like good news from a far country? Time with you is about to stop ; but eternity is near, and it is about to open to you its glories and its joys. You have, perhaps, looked upon the earth from your sick-bed room window for the last time, but in faith and in hope you can now look up, and you see, far up above you, in the calmest, serenest regions of God's great universe, a heaven of life about to open its gates of glory for your joyful reception. You are about to leave dear, loving, sorrowing friends in your chamber of dissolution ; but look up in faith ; dear friends who have formerly left you, and who have entered upon their reward before you, are even now standing upon the shore of Immanuel's land, and are looking forth with enraptured eye that they may see the first glimpse of the ship of salvation rise into view—upon the far-off horizon, in which you are sailing upwards to the haven of eternal glory to join them yonder in their gladness. You are about to pass away from the voice of prayer offered to God for you by your minister, or by some other dear friend, and from the edifying and much-prized religious conversation which these dear ones hold with you, whilst they give expression to their sorrow at parting with you, and to their hope of meeting you again after a short separation. Soon these sounds are to give place to what you will immediately hear, even the high praises of eternity.

You are now on the confines of a glorious eternity, *on the threshold of heaven. You have your trials*—your sorrowful parting with your friends—your heart and flesh beginning to faint and to fail—your soul and your body about to be separated and parted for a season, to enter upon very different portions—the lights that shine upon you whilst upon earth extinguished from your view—the dark night of death beginning to gather in its lowering frown around you. *You have also your comforts.* Jehovah is hearing your prayers in your day of trouble, and is sending you help out of Zion. You hear your Redeemer's voice, in the tones of tenderest love, saying to you, "Fear not; I am the first and the last: I am he that liveth, and was dead; and, behold, I am alive for evermore, Amen; and have the keys of hell and of death." The Holy

Spirit is with you, your light in darkness, your strength in weakness, your joy in sorrow, your peace in believing; and thus you rejoice in the hope of the glory of God. You are leaving your home of love upon earth, the dear friends who are around you in it; but oh! joyous thought, it is to rise and to find prepared for you another in the heavens, where once dear friends, and others who have fallen asleep in Jesus before you, will meet you and salute you as a new member of their family circle with the gush of warmest delight. There they will speak with you, through eternity, in the language of glorified spirits, and dwell with you in love for ever in realms where life never ends and friendship never cools.

I will now endeavour to depict the sorrows and the joys of your present position, by exhibiting to your view others on the threshold and about to enter upon the "Life in Heaven." Contemplate with me the circumstances connected with the death of Moses. View him whilst he lingers on the threshold of glory. His eyes are not dimmed, his strength is not impaired. Even in extreme old age, he retains the full vigour of manhood. The intimation comes out to him from God that he is to leave the Israelites to the care and guidance of Joshua, and to come up to the top of Mount Nebo, there to die before the Lord. The leader of Israel has brought God's covenant-people out of the bondage of Egypt, through the howling wilderness, and has conducted them to the very confines of the promised land. He is not, however, to cross the Jordan, and to put the Israelites in possession of the long-promised inheritance, whom he had for so many years led, and for whom he had so often prayed. He gives them an instructive and a peculiarly appropriate farewell address. He bids them an affecting and tender adieu. He then turns from the congregation, whilst their eyes are steadily fixed upon him; slowly and solemnly he ascends, and ascends alone, to his death-chamber upon the top of a neighbouring, lonely mount. Pensively, but with the most perfect serenity of soul, he reaches its summit. He stands there alone. No human eye is to look in sympathy and in tears upon him whilst his countenance is changing. No human hand is near to minister to his relief. The mountain top is his couch, the stone is his pillow, the sky is the only curtain that throws its folds around his dying bed. He looks around him upon a living world which he is about to leave, and then upwards to a living heaven which he is just about to enter. He looks back and takes another long, affectionate, lingering survey in the direction of the place where the Jewish camp is pitched, and the tents of Israel are spread, with the tabernacle in the midst. He looks onwards towards the west, where the promised land is lying and the Jordan is flowing.

His eye lights on the hill of Tabor, which he is not to tread till he comes down from heaven to meet with Jesus there at the scene of His transfiguration. Eliezer is not present to put up a prayer for him, that he might be supported and comforted; he utters a secret prayer that God may shield him in his solitude, and receive his redeemed spirit up and home to heaven. Moses is now done with the earth and with all sublunary affairs. He stretches himself upon the cold ground, he closes his eyes upon all that is visible, and looks up silently in faith upon the opening invisibilities that are above. In patience and holy submission he waits God's time when his spirit is to mount and enter his Father's home in glory. He waits not long. God lays His finger upon his heart; in a moment its action ceases; the pulse stops; the cold benumbing feeling of death begins to spread through every part of the body; he dies before the Lord; his soul rises and enters heaven. Thus, from his friendless death-couch upon the lonely mount, he ascends and mingles, still in life, with God's great family above.

Look now at the patriarch Jacob "on the threshhold." He meets death in very different circumstances. His children and friends are around him. Jacob has spent a long and an eventful life upon earth, and whilst the evening shades calmly and cloudlessly begin to gather around him, he dies as many a parent has died—in the bosom of his family circle. He knows his departure is at hand, either by divine intimation, or by the feeling of his increasing weakness. He sends for his children and friends to come and see him before he die, that he may pray for them, and implore God's blessing to descend upon them. Jacob's death-chamber is pregnant with interest to every head of a family when stretched, in the providence of God, upon a dying bed. There is not another death-bed scene so full of example recorded in the Bible. Jacob knew that the words of the dying have been looked upon as sacred in every age, find an entrance at once into the hearts of the mourners around, and often are powerfully instrumental, by the blessing of the Spirit of God, in awakening the careless and in edifying those in a state of grace. Jacob accordingly assembles his household around his dying bed; he gives to his children successively such exhortations as their circumstances required; and with fond wishes and many prayers, and with the hope of yet meeting them in heaven, where death and separation are unknown, he commits them to God. He is happy in his own spiritual experience, and his soul is comforted by the great and glorious realities of the future that are opening upon his view. He has long experienced the covenant mercies of his God. Now he feels that God is indeed the portion of his soul, the eternal God is his refuge, and around him are the everlasting arms.

The Angel of the covenant has spread around him the pavilion of His love, with the light, and peacefulness, and solace of His own gracious presence. He looks up in faith and sees the peopled heavens above, throwing open for his reception the everlasting doors, that he may enter more than a conqueror over death, and find there a home of love for eternity. He hears the voice that calls him home; his response is, "I have waited for thy salvation, O Lord." He is in the possession of the most perfect consciousness—the whole scene bears evidence of this; he looks up from his family and friends assembled around him in his dying chamber, to the great family of God, and whom he is just about to join: his last prayer is offered, he ceases to speak, his work on earth is done, he is on the threshold of another life, he draws his feet up into the bed. Those around in speechless silence look on; and behold the work of the Lord, the change which death produces. Lo! the pallor of dissolution is upon the countenance; the eyes are suddenly, and as if somewhat painfully, turned up, and become fixed in the upward, vacant, sightless gaze of death; the bosom no longer heaves, it is at rest and is still; the last quiver has passed from the lips. Jacob is already seated in the chariot of salvation. The path to glory is entered upon; and surrounded by a bright and rejoicing convoy of attending angels, he leaves the earth and rises to his reward. "Let me die the death of the righteous, and let my last end be like his."

How varying and vastly different are the circumstances of God's children, when, in His holy providence with them, they are brought face to face with death, and are placed "on the threshold." Come with me in imagination to the hill of Calvary, and in the painful and bloody death of the penitent malefactor, there you witness a scene very different indeed from the peacefulness and love of Jacob's death-chamber. Lo! you see upon a cross, near to which the Son of God is bleeding, a malefactor nailed in all the agony of crucifixion. He lived a careless and wicked life; till at last arrested by the hand of justice, he is condemned by the laws of his country to die. Thus he hangs, outwardly writhing in pain, and bathed with blood,—inwardly impenitent, his heart hard and his conscience unawakened; for at first he frowns in his impenitence upon Jesus, and joins those who revile the meek and lowly Sufferer. At last his eye turns from surveying the insulting Jews, lights wonderingly and gazingly upon the face of Jesus, so calm in pain, so placid in the enduring of almost unbearable sorrows. Jesus prays. How does that prayer, by its very sweetness, tenderness, and charity, startle him! Jesus has been injured, betrayed, arraigned, unrighteously condemned, is enduring uncomplainingly an unmerited death. The Jews are His enemies without a cause. What, then, is His prayer? It is not that God would make bare His holy arm for their signal and immediate punishment; it is not for vengeance upon His relentless persecutors. The voice of Jesus—sweet, loving, and mild—rises to the Father in the words, "Father, forgive them; for they know not what they do." In that prayer of Jesus, the malefactor hears something that is above nature; there is in it the voice Divine,—the very long-suffering and endurance of a God of mercy. The mild heat of the summer sun melts the snow and thaws the ice. The love and forgiving spirit of Jesus melts that man's heart; and, bursting into tears of contrition, he looks full into Christ's face, all bathed with blood, and exclaims, "Lord, remember me when thou comest into thy kingdom." The cry of supplication never reaches Christ's ear in vain. The answer is immediately given, "Verily I say unto thee, To-day shalt thou be with me in paradise." There may be but few death-bed repentances. It may be true that *generally* people die just as they live. Still, God's grace is all-sufficient, and we believe is not restrained until the last spark of expiring life goes out. And here is an instance of at least *one* individual becoming a penitent when on the threshold of a dark and lowering and unprovided-for eternity. Now he can look up to God as a Father reconciled, to Jesus as his Saviour, to the Holy Spirit as his life and spiritual portion, to heaven as his home. He has now *the prospect* that his sufferings will all terminate on this side of the veil; and that when he rises at death from viewing the great assemblages whom he beholds crowding the hill of Calvary, he will enter heaven, and see around him there the larger assemblies of the skies, and hear them, not reviling the Son of God, but proclaiming of Him, "Thou wast slain, and hast redeemed us to God by thy blood." The now lifeless body, bathed with blood, and wet with the tears of a late repentance, is left hanging upon the cross. The soul, however, redeemed by Christ's blood, and sanctified by His Spirit, takes its flight upwards towards heaven. Jesus is already there,—receives him home, a welcome pilgrim from the hill of Calvary, probably the *first* soul saved by His blood after it was actually shed.

CHAPTER VI.

ON THE THRESHOLD—(*continued.*)

LOOK now upon another of God's children "on the threshold," dying, not in his bed, with assembled and sympathising friends around him, but laid at the rich man's gate, and there left to perish, unpitied by human eye, and unrelieved by human hand. Look first at the mansion to which that gate leads. Its towering battlements and lofty pillars, standing sentry in their massiveness on each side of the door, give evidence that it is the home of one of the grandees of earth. Listen! there is within the melody of the sweetest music, and, in addition, the sound of dancing and of revelry is falling upon your ear. The lighted tapers are throwing their stream of illumination far and wide around them upon the lowering pavilion of night. All is light, and gladsomeness, and frolic within that gay dwelling. But, lo! what a different scene is transacting at the gate. Lazarus is lying there, unheeded and unpitied, and is sinking under the weight of years and of trouble. His eyes are already glazed; his lips are pale and parched, but no friendly hand is near to moisten them; the cold sweat of death is falling in many a drop from his furrowed brow; the convulsively heavy breathing is bearing its voiceless testimony that the sand-glass of life is nearly run. This is transacting upon earth. What is happening in heaven? There is a thrill of sympathetic feeling streaming through the bosoms of its inhabitants towards that poor beggar who is dying so destitute and unpitied at yonder gate. God has already given the command to those ministering spirits, who hear His voice in heaven and hearken to His word, to go down to that gate and bring Lazarus home. They have already given obedience; their passage from heaven to earth is effected; they are hovering on their wings of light and of love around that dying saint, waiting till the redeemed spirit issues into their midst, when it quits the changed body. This at last takes place. These angels receive the spirit of Lazarus, and close around him. How do they immediately act? They tarry not to look in upon the dancers at the hall, nor to listen to their music, nor to bury the diseased body; their glad assemblage is instantly in motion; they spread forth, with a rustle, their wings of love and of joy upon the evening air, and, bearing homewards to Abraham's bosom the sainted spirit, they return to their native heavens.

Come now with me and be witness of a different death-scene,—Stephen "on the threshold," put to death by the hand of violence. What a distressing spectacle opens to our view! You have perhaps never seen a human being ruthlessly put to death by the hand of his fellow-man; but you can realise what is taking place at Stephen's death if you have mingled with the crowd and looked upon a condemned prisoner suffering death upon the scaffold. Have you seen a prisoner, pinioned and pale, issue from the precincts of the prison, and amid the solemnities of the day of execution take his place upon the apparatus of death? What a thrill of breathless emotion streams through your bosom as you gaze upon the haggard countenance and upon the restless eyes of the criminal about to be executed, looking down upon the assembled masses of spectators stretching far and near, before and around the scaffold! Have you witnessed the minister of the gospel, Heaven's ambassador of peace to man, finish his prayer, step aside, and leave the prisoner at the very gate of death? Have you looked upon the executioner then step forward to perform his part in the awful tragedy—slip the rope around the neck of the trembling victim, draw the fatal cap over his eyes, place in his hand the death-signal, and retire? Have you felt your heart throb, your eyes grow dim, your limbs shake, your breathing become choked, as you gazed upon the man, hooded now and shut out from all that is visible, pausing for a few terrible moments upon the threshold of an awful eternity before he takes his leap out of time into the great unseen? Oh, the fall of the drop, instantly followed by the dash downwards and the recoiling swing of the man, choking and convulsively heaving in the agonies of death, have an effect upon the souls of the spectators which even the stoutest heart can scarcely endure!

In Stephen's martyrdom you see a death as violent, but more lawless and tumultuous. He is not arraigned and condemned by a regular process of law, and then carried forth in solemnity along the stern path of justice to suffer the punishment which the law prescribes. Lo! he is near the beautiful gate of the temple; there is around him a crowd of Jews in a state of strange and frantic excitement. How calm Stephen is! how serene and sweet his aspect! his face in a blaze of glory shining like that of an angel! He kneels down and prays to the God of his salvation to succour him in this trying hour, to shield him in the last alarm, to stretch forth from heaven the arms of His love, and to enfold him in the embrace of His covenant protection.

The first pitiless stone is thrown; it strikes Stephen with that soft, dull, and heavy crash that falls so distressingly and gratingly upon the ear. Stones follow in rapid succession. Stephen at first is kneeling in prayer, with his hands clasped, and his eyes upraised to heaven; but, like ripened grain beat down by the descending hail, he falls upon his back and lies stretched upon the ground, his bruised and bleeding body starting with convulsive twitchings.

Even in this awful situation he feels on the very threshold. The heavens above him are opened to his view, and, looking upwards into them, he sees a different spectacle from that which is around him upon earth: "But he, being full of the Holy Ghost, looked up stedfastly into heaven, and saw the glory of God, and Jesus standing on the right hand of God, and said, Behold, I see the heavens opened, and the Son of man standing on the right hand of God." How comforting is this view to the dying saint! Heaven opening its doors of love, that he may enter it to find there an everlasting home! God in His glory upon the throne, Jesus at the Father's right hand risen up in His sympathy, ready with outstretched arms to welcome Stephen in! The chariot of salvation, encircled by shining angels, near and already prepared, in which he is to rise to the realms of eternal day and into his everlasting reward! Stephen dies with the words of prayer upon his lips, "Lord Jesus, receive my spirit!"

Without referring further to the dying experience whilst on the threshold of those whose names are mentioned in the Bible, I will now introduce the religious views and hopes of some others of the children of God when in the same position. Here is the recorded experience of one :—

"'I feel almost overwhelmed, when I think on what I am to be, and what I am to see. When shall "the day break, and the shadows flee away? Turn, my beloved, and be thou like to a roe, or to a young hart upon the mountains of Bether." I am longing to be dissolved, and "to be with Christ, which is far better."'

"Then he said, 'Oh let us exalt His name together. Oh glory dwells in Immanuel's land. I long for the fragrancy of the spiced wine. Stay me with flagons; comfort me with apples, for I am sick of love.'

"'Glory to Him. What shall I render to God! let us exalt His name together; He has done wonderful things for me. I shall be in heaven shortly, by the blood of the Lamb. In heaven we shall have a more glorious and abiding sight of Christ than on the mount of transfiguration. We shall behold His glory; we shall be made like Him, for we shall see Him as He is.'

"When his soul appeared, as it were, just on the verge of the New Jerusalem, many sweet and heavenly expressions dropped from his lips, among which were the following: 'Glory to God,' said he, 'in the highest, that there is goodwill to men, and peace on earth; glory, that life and immortality is brought to light. Help to put a crown on the Mediator's head. It will be our glory to eternity to run deeper and deeper in debt. Glory to God that a vile worm, the chief of sinners, is singled out to be a monument of His grace, and a trumpeter of His praise.'

"'Here you see a man dying a monument of the glorious power of admirable, astonishing grace; and generations to come shall call *me* blessed. Follow my advice, study the power of religion; it is the *power* of religion, and not *a name* that will give the comfort I find. And if there be such a glory in His conduct to me now, oh, what will it be in that day, to see the Lamb *that was slain* in the midst of the throne?' And some of the last words he was heard to utter were, 'Not I, but the grace of God in me. I am near the crown I have been wrestling for so long. Free grace! free grace! Not unto me, not unto me be the glory.' Shortly after he had spoken these words, his happy spirit winged its flight to the land *where the weary are at rest.*"

Here is the religious experience of a mother when "on the threshold":—

"For several weeks before her removal, she could take but little rest, and was unable to remain in any other than an upright position.

"When one of her children noticed the progress of the disease on her enfeebled frame, she said, 'I am only so much nearer home: a little more suffering, and the weary wheels of life will stand still. There will be a host of glorified saints, whom I have known on earth, to welcome me on that celestial shore.'

"Some refreshment being offered her, she remarked that every thing on earth to her had lost its relish. After this, she sat for a short time in silence; then, breaking forth in the most ecstatic joy, she cried aloud, 'Jesus! Jesus! oh, do not you see Him? There He is, with His five bleeding wounds, which were received on Calvary for me, for me!' Speaking to her husband shortly after, she said, 'Oh, I have had a delightful view of the heavenly road; my Saviour is at the end of it, beckoning me away. How thin the partition wall between me and the inhabitants of heaven!' It had been her earnest prayer, during her long and painful affliction, that her mental composure might not be disturbed. And her prayer was answered. She was perfectly collected to the last. But a few minutes before she expired, one of her daughters observed, 'It is hard toiling:' she added, 'to make the blest shore.' Shortly after, she took her flight from the earthly tabernacle, and entered into that heavenly rest which she had so long and so joyfully anticipated."

I will only refer to the dying experience of another believer when "on the threshold," who exultingly rejoiced in the hope of the glory of God:—

"When he fell into a decline, and was fully aware that he had little prospect of recovering, he was far from being alarmed. 'I am ashamed,' he said, 'to desire and pray for life. Is there anything here more desirable than the enjoyment of Jesus Christ? Can I desire anything below comparable to that blessed vision? O that crown! that rest which remains for the people of God! and, blessed be God, I can say I know it is mine!'

"To a friend who visited him, and who spoke of the excellency of Christ, and of the glory of the invisible world, he replied, 'Ah! I feel something of it. My heart is as full as it can hold in this lower state.'

"'Oh, why should any of you be so sad while I am so very happy! This, this is the hour that I have waited for!'

"A short time before his death, he said, 'Come, let us lift up our voice in praise. I have nothing else to do. I have done with prayer and all other ordinances. I have almost done conversing with mortals; I shall presently behold Christ himself, who died for me, and loved me, and washed me in His blood. I shall in a few hours be in eternity, singing the song of Moses, and the song of the Lamb. I shall presently stand upon Mount Sion, with an innumerable company of angels, and the spirits of just men made perfect, and Jesus the Mediator of the new covenant. I shall hear the voice of much people, and be one among them who say, "Hallelujah! Salvation, glory, and honour, and power, be unto the Lord our God!" And again we say, "Hallelujah!" Methinks I stand as it were with one foot in heaven and the other on earth. Methinks I hear the melody of heaven, and by faith I see the angels waiting to carry my soul to be for ever with the Lord in glory.'"

Reader! dost thou wish when thy last sickness has come, and when thou art laid upon a bed of dissolution, to lie there "on the threshold" of an eternity of glory? Live *mindful* of this; and let thy present life be the preparation for it. It is "A STATE OF GRACE UPON EARTH THAT IS THE ONLY PREPARATION FOR A STATE OF GLORY IN HEAVEN." It is a life spent in preparing for heaven, through the faith of the Son of God, that will usher thee at death into its glories and its joys.

CHAPTER VII.

THE WAY BY WHICH GOD'S CHILDREN ENTER HEAVEN.

GOD'S children, by the appointment of their Father, enter heaven through the pathway of temporal death. The passage is thus a dark and a dismal one that conducts believers up into heaven—the world of life and of light. Temporal death to man is not a *necessary* consequence flowing out of the very possession of life—such as the withering of the leaf upon the tree is a necessary consequence of the approach of autumn. Death to man is not a *necessity*, it is the judicial appointment of God because of sin; it is one of the *consequences* of sin, which the death of Christ has not removed, even in the case of believers.

There was a time when death did not exist in any world of the great empire over which the God of life reigns. Then an unfading and unwithering summer of life shone upon every portion of the *great universe of* God. From His throne of life in these high heavens God looked down upon his intelligent creation, all in a glow of life and of health; and wherever His eye wandered, He beheld neither the blight nor the dark shadow either of temporal, spiritual, or of eternal death—no death-bed, no funeral procession, no mournful and lonely grave. It is strange that heaven was the first world in God's great universe into which death found an entrance; for the *first sin* was committed in heaven, when a large number of the angels of God *through* sin lost their place in glory, and sunk into a state of spiritual and of eternal death. Sin is the cause of death. Sin is the troubled and muddy fountain; death is the dark, and cold, and sullen stream;—sin puts out the light, blows out the candle, extinguishes the sun of life that shines upon us from the sky of our existence; death is the dark night that consequently and naturally follows.

God made man but a little lower than the angels, and crowned him with glory and honour. God placed our first parents in Eden to wear, during their probation season there, the crown of immortality—a crown that was to encircle their brows for ever in unfading beauty. Even had our first parents resisted Satan's temptation when he came sneaking upon his mission of seduction into Eden—the paradise of flowers, and of life, and of joy—Eden, I believe, would not have been their eternal home. Our first parents were placed in Eden in a state of *probation.* Probation means a course of trial and of exertion, with the object of securing a reward, or of rising to a higher position than the state in which the probationer is placed. That reward in the case of the human family—had man not fallen—would have been a translation to heaven without tasting of death, and the enjoyment of endless blessedness there, when the appointed season of probation here had terminated. Thus, had our first parents kept their covenant with God, the earth would not have been their everlasting habitation; their probation state in Eden implies that God had destined them for a state that was higher. Had they resisted the tempter, at the appointed time, when God was to confer upon them their reward, He would have taken them up, as He did Enoch and Elijah, with their soul and body unseparated, into heaven, to dwell throughout eternity in His glorious and manifested presence there, and to mingle and associate with angels in the world of life above us, for ever and ever.

How delightful would life have been, if we had been privileged to live during our probation season in the world, free from all anxiety, and from every kind of trouble and sickness and trial, blooming in the glow of unchanging health and of immortal youth, and had then been permitted to leave it without suffering death at all! Life with us in that case would have been all summer, a sky without a cloud: no frost would have breathed upon the flowers of immortality to wither and crumple their leaves: no night of death, in its sable gloom and silence and dreary desolation, would have darkened over us, and come down upon our changed countenances and closed eyes and desolated homes. How delightful would it have been to meet our friends when God appointed our separation from them, not by death, but by a glorious translation up into heaven, into a state of high and holy and exalted blessedness there! We would in that case have felt, at the time of our departure from the world, exactly in the position of the emigrant, when leaving his friends and his native land to go out into a distant country. Before the emigrant sails, he meets his friends; he speaks with them about the country to which he is to set sail; he gives them the promise that he will remember them when he has reached the land of his adoption; that when upon its distant shores he will write to them, and let them know his opinion of the country, of its inhabitants, of its institutions, of its customs; and will let them know from time to time how he is getting on; and will give them a hearty welcome when they follow him, and join him in his new home. The emigrant at last bids these friends adieu, not to go out of existence, but merely to go forth alive into the land that lies far off: he shakes hands with them, and embarks; the ship moves off; he stands upon the deck; he looks back upon the receding and lessening forms of these friends standing upon the shore, whose white handkerchiefs are fluttering in the air, and are waving him a kind adieu. The friends upon the shore follow, with their anxious look, the vessel receding on the bosom of the ocean, becoming apparently smaller and smaller, till at last, like a mere speck upon the far-off horizon, it suddenly flits from their view. The friend they love, who is in the vessel, does not pass out of existence when they lose sight of him, but merely beyond the reach of their vision and of their voice.

If temporal death, through sin, had not entered into the world, Christ's glorious ascension to heaven would have been an exemplification of the way in which all God's children would have entered it. On the mount of Olivet, Jesus meets His assembled disciples and followers. He makes this joyful announcement to them, "All power is given unto me in heaven and in earth." He lifts up His holy hands to heaven; He blesses them. It comes to pass, while He is in the act of blessing them, He is parted from them, and is carried up into heaven.

The emigrant embarks, sails over the bosom of the ocean, stops not in his voyage till he reaches the land whither he is bound, and there disembarks upon its shore. At His ascension, Jesus passes over the bosom of that expanse, or rather ocean, of space, that intervenes betwixt earth and heaven, enters these high and glorious courts with His *human* soul and human body united, and these again in union with the Divine nature, and sits down for eternity upon the throne with God.

This is exactly what would have taken place at the time of our departure from the world had our first parents stood firm in the covenant of their God. Oh ! had this been the destiny of the whole human family, what different scenes we would now be daily witnessing ! Not the window-blinds drawn down to shut out the joyful light of the sun from that sick chamber, where a poor dying patient is laid upon a bed of trouble, and is enduring there the moanings of pain, the tossings of great distress, —not the doctor hurrying past us towards that sick chamber, to endeavour either entirely to remove, or at least to alleviate, by the aid of medicine, the sufferings of that poor invalid,—not the minister, the messenger of peace, passing slowly and solemnly and pensively along to the same home, to administer consolation and good hope through grace, through our reigning and now glorified Redeemer; and this not only to the sick individual, but also to the sympathising mourners who are gathered around,—not the sorrowful meeting on the funeral day in the house of mourning, the gloomy hearse, with its nodding plumes, and the dark and sable attendants, passing on to perform the last sad office of friendship to the departed, but still beloved dead, when man goes to his long home, and the mourners go about the streets,—not the mourning attendants standing around the newly opened grave whilst letting down the coffin, with a dear but changed friend in it, into its narrow, dark, cold, and silent resting-place, there to sleep apart from a living world till Christ come the second time, till the resurrection morning dawn. Instead of such scenes as these, which now meet our eye oft and oft in this vale of tears, we would, day after day, have seen the sky above us dotted here and there with another and another of the children of God, whose probation season on earth was finished, flying up without tasting of death to heaven, like a moving cloud of joy, and as the doves to their windows.

Image in these circumstances what would have taken place in your home at the departure of a beloved parent. Realise the ascension of your mother to heaven, for example, without tasting of death ; and this would have been the way the whole members of the human family would have left the world if man had not fallen. Image your being called to meet your beloved mother in your home—the home she is about to leave, for she has received intimation from God that the time has come when she is to leave earth and rise and enter heaven. You, her beloved children, stand round about her, as the disciples stood round about Jesus upon the mount of Olives. You are listening to her farewell address, as the assembled Israelites listened, in breathless silence, to the affecting farewell exhortation which Moses delivered to them just *before* his ascension to the mount, from the top of which his redeemed and glorified spirit took its flight up into the opening, densely-peopled, and glorious heavens. You cling fondly to her side whilst she yet remains; you anxiously watch, in trembling anxiety, for the sign of her departing, which she is about to give you, such as the quiet recognising look, or the gentle wave of her pale hand after it has been lifted up to implore God's blessing upon you; her feet already lightly press the step in the front of your door; she is about to rise; her eyes, suffused with tears, and somewhat dimmed by the thought of parting, are lifted up; her hands and her arms are outstretched, like the wings of a dove about to mount upwards; and her shining face is already radiant with the descending light of a glorious eternity. Lo! now her feet no longer press that stone at your door-step; she is already in motion; she is rising slowly and majestically above your home; the separation is effected; she is going up from your home, and is on her way to enter the home of her Father in heaven. In silence you raise your eye, dim with the sorrow of separation, upwards after her, ascending higher and higher, as relatives on shore gaze after a receding vessel, carrying away a friend, with its white sails outspread upon the bosom of the ocean. Your mother is upon her voyage to enter a glorious eternity. She is in your view becoming smaller and smaller, till at last she dwindles into the form of a small contracting cloudlet upon the face of the clear, high, and seemingly far-distant sky. Your mother is disappearing from the field of *your* vision, but she is *rising* into the view of the glorious hosts of heaven, who are looking forth upon her from the door-steps of eternity and from the windows of heaven in their joy, and are all exultant and glad to welcome her home. Your ascending and dearly beloved mother is already high and far away beyond the reach of your voice; but, hark! what cry, what commingled ocean of voices is that which is now rolling down upon *her* listening ear? It is the welcoming acclaim of ten thousand times ten thousand, and thousands of thousands, who are looking down upon her ascent in a flutter of emotional gladness, and are longing for her arrival to join them in a glorious and blissful eternity. She is emerging out of the mists and out of the dark nights of time, and is rising into their enraptured view, and their joyous cry above her, and over her, and around her, is, "Lift up your heads, O ye gates, even lift them up, ye everlasting doors;" "Come in, thou blessed of the Lord." The Father's welcome is, "Come up hither, come and see." Christ's welcome from the mediatorial throne is, "Well done, good and faithful servant, enter thou into the joy of thy Lord." Your dear mother is now away from you; her home upon earth is left; her chair is empty; she is gone; she has left you as Enoch and Elijah left the world, and she has entered heaven without tasting of death.

Image to yourself this other parting scene. I am about to lose a beloved child, not by death, but by her translation to heaven,—marriage is not an arrangement adopted by God subsequent to the fall; marriage would have existed had man never fallen; it existed betwixt our first parents whilst they were yet in a state of innocency,—my dear child is not to die, but she is to be taken from me by God, in the glad morning of life, like a rose plucked from the bush when in the bud not yet blown; she is to be taken up into the garden of God's glory; and thus, to my beloved one, the less of earth, the more of heaven—the less of time, the more of an eternity of glory. Oh, I can conceive that if this had been the *way* in which the unfallen children of the human family had been received by God up into heaven, I would, at the moment of separation from my dearly beloved child, have fondly and lovingly, but at the same time with a spirit of the holiest resignation to the will of my Father, clasped her, warm in all the glow of life, and blooming in all the flush of beauty and of health; for mark, she is not dead, she is not cold; she is not in the condition of the daughter of Jairus lying in her father's home, with her countenance changed, her pulse stopped, and her bosom at rest; she is not in the condition of Sarah when Abraham rises up, in the land of the stranger, to bury his dead out of his sight, and to commit her cold remains to the cold earth, who has long been his beloved partner and companion in the journey of life.

My parting from the fair child I am about to lose—if man had not fallen—would have been a very different scene. I see her radiant with the flush of a joyful immortality. She was never sick; she is not appointed to die; the stamp of a new life is upon her soul; the bloom of immortality is upon her countenance: the rose upon her cheek appears as if its leaves were wet with the dews of an eternal morning,—shining beneath the descending light of an unsetting sun: the lily, in its delicate paleness and purity, encircles her brow; and the light of peace and sanctified affection is in her eye,—these eyes that are like two morning stars quietly shining out from a pure, cloudless sky, when beheld in Italian climes,—eyes that are never to be closed in death.

The moment of separation is come. That lovely child takes us by the hand. Suddenly, and somewhat exultingly, and, at the same time, with a subdued tone of voice and faltering accent, as if a sudden cloud of passing sorrow had flitted over her exultant spirit, she says, "Oh! my dear earthly parents, adieu, a fond adieu! Lo! my heavenly Father is looking down upon me from yonder glad and holy heaven, where saints immortal reign. He is waiting for my arrival in the bright realms of eternal day. He is already in motion to welcome *me home.* Lo! He is stretching out His arms to embrace me. His smile, the sweet smile of a loving father, is upon me. Oh! He is longing with all a father's tenderness to receive me up into yon joyous home of love, and to join yon great and glad family who are praising *their* Father and *my* Father before His throne."

She gives us a parting kiss. She suddenly looks round the room, that she may take a last and a farewell survey of it, in which we are met, holding sweet and holy converse previous to our separation and her ascension. That lovely child, who is so dear to us who are around her, feels a heavenly attraction operating upon her, an impulse from above, that impels her to ascend. She rises somewhat suddenly. She breathes, sweetly and calmly, "Adieu! adieu! We will soon meet again up *yonder!*—for our heavenly Father will soon call upon you also, my dearly beloved friends, to rise from earth and come up to heaven: ye will follow me; and we will meet again, and be happy for eternity."

I see her now as she lingers for a moment upon the step, for, with all her desire to depart, she still feels for us whom she is about to leave. She looks up to heaven, whilst her eyes are full of holiness and love; and her face, even as that of an angel, seems already taking on the descending reflection of heaven's own glory; her golden ringlets floating in many a graceful curl upon the air are like a rainbow of beauty, throwing its arch of loveliness around her neck. She lifts her hand, and gently waves it, as if saying to those up in heaven, who are looking down upon her, watching her every movement, and longing for her to rise and join them, "I am just coming." She takes the last look of that sun that is shining so resplendently above her in the sky, as if it were the bright gateway which is to afford her an entrance into the glorious heaven of light which she is about to enter: she takes the last look of the gay green earth, in whose bosom there is not a grave, and from whose surface there rises not a sigh to the ear of the glad and listening heavens. She surveys its grassy plains and its wooded hills, and its sparkling streams: she takes the last look of her youthful home in which she was born, and in which she has, through her covenant communion with God, experienced an earnest and a foretaste of those joys that are at His right hand, and of those pleasures above that shall endure for evermore: she turns and gazes pensively and lovingly into our faces, for she feels almost an unfondness yet to leave us: her face turned upon us, though in a glow of holy delight, is yet shaded and slightly clouded at the thought of parting,—like a bright sky, with a few fleecy clouds sprinkled here and there upon its calm, sweet face. We start forward almost involuntarily again to shake hands ere we part, and again to bid her another fond and lingering adieu. *Oh, are* we too late! she has already risen; her little foot no longer presses the court at the front of our door. She is away!—she is away! A cloud of accompanying angels is around her, and they are soaring upwards towards the bright heavens: she has spread forth, upon the ocean expanse that stretches far away, the sails of faith, love, hope, holy desire, and a heavenly breathing after glory: she is upon the bosom of a cloud ascending to heaven. That fair child has now left our home upon earth; but she is not away from us to be a homeless wanderer over the wide wastes of a desolate eternity: she is rising, and is already entering the home of our Father in heaven: she has left our presence and company; but she is already away to enjoy the company of her God, and to follow the Lamb whithersoever He goeth: she hears not now our voice, but up yonder above her in the peopled heavens, which she is just about to enter, listens to the sweet-toned roll of angels' songs, and the holy praises of glorified saints: she is looking not now upon our upturned faces; for she has higher attractions: she sees God, she sees Jesus, she sees the Holy Spirit, she sees angels, she sees the masses of the glorified, who are glittering far and near in their robes of white: she feels upon her spirit the summer glow of her heavenly Father's smile; the everlasting arms are around her: she is enfolded in His covenant embrace: she is home, *she is home!*

CHAPTER VIII.

THE WAY BY WHICH GOD'S CHILDREN ENTER HEAVEN—(*continued.*)

HOW delightful would this world have been, and how joyful would it have been to leave it, if God, at the end of our probation season here, had thus received us up into heaven, without suffering death! In this case, when the time of my departure arrived, I would have bidden my friends, my acquaintances, and the dear ones, adieu, who form my home loved circle. I would, healthy, and well, and buoyant, with the glow of immortality upon my brow, have shaken hands with them, and committed them in prayer to God, and have parted with them, not as I must do now at my death—for death is in the world through sin—to have my countenance changed, and my eyes closed in a long unbroken sleep, and my face becoming so rigid, and cold, and far away, and fixed in its expression, that my warmest and most loving friends are forced to cover it so as to hide it from their view, and to have my body put into the narrow and dreary coffin, (to be committed on the funeral day to the deep, and cold, and silent grave,) there to rest in its dreamless repose, apart from a living world, and there to sleep, till awakened by the dawning upon my lonely bed of the great morning of eternity, and by the loud, terrible blast of the archangel's trumpet, calling upon the long-forgotten dead to rise. Then only will I come up out of my long hiding-place, and looking around me will see the whole world in a bustle, for the resurrection of the dead is taking place, and all is in a state of commotion over the surface of the whole earth; then, my soul reunited with my upraised body, I will rise and enter into heaven.

Instead of this, I would have risen up from the earth without tasting of death, and would, with my body and soul never to be separated, have ascended to the realms of eternal day.

It is not, however, in this way that the children of God now enter into heaven; it is along the dark pathway of temporal death. God has delivered believers both from spiritual, and also from eternal death. Here is an important question, Why did God not proceed just one step further, and deliver them in addition from the stroke of temporal death,—the shock of a painful dissolution? When we look at God's dealings with *some* of the human family, it appears perfectly evident, as I have stated, that there is no *absolute* and un-

avoidable necessity that we should suffer temporal death at all. Had God so ordained, we who believe might have been exempted from temporal, just as we are freed from spiritual and eternal death. Thus, when we had finished our probation season in this world, we might have left it, and have entered heaven, as our eternal home, without the endurance of sickness, and without sinking under the pall of temporal dissolution. We see this evidenced and exemplified in the case of *two* members of the human family.

During the existence of the patriarchal dispensation, Enoch, the seventh from Adam, is translated to heaven without suffering temporal death at all: "Enoch walked with God: and he was not; for God took him." "By faith Enoch was translated that he should not see death, and was not found, because God had translated him; for before his translation he had this testimony, that he pleased God." Enoch's soul does not enter heaven to live there and to rejoice there in a widowed state, amid its living realities, and its crowding assemblies, and its eternal glories, whilst his body is lying in the cold grave, and is encircled with the silent solemnities of death. With soul and body unseparated, Enoch rises in his chariot of salvation, and enters heaven, and meets God, and dwells with God.

I see a similar exemption from temporal death vouchsafed by God to another of His children, during the existence of the Mosaic economy. The prophet Elijah does not die, he enters heaven without tasting death: "And it came to pass, as they still went on, and talked, that, behold, there appeared a chariot of fire, and horses of fire, and parted them both asunder; and Elijah went up by a whirlwind into heaven. And Elisha saw it, and he cried, My father, my father, the chariot of Israel, and the horsemen thereof." Elijah ascended in these circumstances, with his body and soul unseparated, and entered into glory. He and Enoch now exhibit to the spirits of the just made perfect, what they are to become after the resurrection morning has dawned.

If God *could*, in consistency with the great principles of His moral government, thus exempt and deliver *two* members of the human family from temporal death, He could, upon the same principles, have delivered *all* who are His children, had it been His holy and blessed will, and had He seen it to be proper. Why then, it may be asked, did God not grant a similar exemption from temporal death to all who are believers in Christ Jesus? There must be *some* reason why God does not do this. The *reason* of this, however, is one of those secret things which belong to the Lord our God; it has not been revealed to us in His holy Word. I venture, however, to give this supposition. The universal reign of death shews two things—*first, The malignity of sin; second, Our need of a Saviour.* God may see the universal reign of temporal death to be necessary to convince us of sin, that the whole world is guilty before God. Had God exempted believers from temporal death, and subjected the impenitent to it, this would have anticipated the public award of the judgment-day; besides, men might, in this case, have rashly inferred that this exemption from temporal death happened because believers had no sin; as it is, believers are prevented from rashly inferring their acceptance by God in the Beloved, without the possession of Christ's moral image upon their soul, for they *die* as well as the wicked; and, further, Jesus died and went down into the cold grave, and thus believers only walk the path which Jesus trod before them, when they suffer temporal death.

God allows temporal death to reign both over the righteous and the wicked, to shew us what sin really is, to convince us that sin is the *cause* of death, that sin is of *terrible malignity*, that there is thus the *more* need to betake ourselves, with all urgency and earnestness, to Christ, the remedy. Further, grim and grisly death, gaunt, stern, and horrible, seen standing and heard knocking at every door, is the very means of awakening a sleeping world. All do not hear the voice of the preacher of the gospel, and do not feel the knockings of God's Word as a hammer upon their hard and flinty hearts; but all hear the voice of death speaking to them in God's dispensations with others, as well as with themselves, and feel the influence upon their souls of its awakening terrors. View death as coming to the dying through sin, as its cause, and you thus see, in a way you can scarcely do otherwise, your need of an interest in Jesus, whose blood cleanseth from all sin. View the hour of death as hid, and when it will come uncertain, and this is calculated to awaken us to a right improvement of time. View death as certain and assuredly coming, whether we make preparation for it or not, and this shews us the necessity of instantly shaking ourselves free from a spirit of carelessness and sloth, and fleeing by faith to Jesus.

Careless as the world is, it would be more so if temporal death did not exist, and did not continue in its sable vestments to preach its terrible sermon about sin to those who are in it. Temporal death proclaims to us, in a voice that cannot be misunderstood, the startling *fact* that sin is no trifle in the view of God whatever it may be in ours, for it is the *cause* of the tremendous change which temporal death produces. The existence of temporal death is also a ceaseless monitor urging us to flee to Jesus, who, having taken the sting from death and wrenched the victory from the grave, enables us, in holy triumph, to say, "O death, where is thy sting? O grave, where is thy victory?" There is no such impressive sermon preached as that which falls upon our ear from the dark pulpit of the sick-chamber, the death-bed, the newly opened grave. Listen to that sermon, learn its awful announcement about sin, and flee to the stronghold.

A WORD TO THE IMPENITENT.

Death to you, if you continue to reject the offer of salvation made to you by a merciful God, and to trifle with your eternal interests, will be the way along which your disembodied soul will pass that it may enter hell. Awake, thou that sleepest! Flee from coming wrath! Is the consideration of your death a subject that gives you pain, and do you thus shut out the thought of it as much as possible from your mind? You may shut out the thought of Death, and you may continue to dance thoughtlessly and laughingly along the flowery path of life, but I beg to remind you that this will not keep him away. He will come whether you think about him or not. He will come whether or not you betake yourselves by faith to Jesus, who has conquered him and wrenched the victory from the grave. When the Lord Jesus, who is upon the throne, gives the commission to the dark angel to pay you a visit, and to end your present connexion with the world, and to lead you out of time into eternity, he will not linger and wait at your door until you have awakened out of your spiritual slumber, and have rubbed your opening eyes, and have brushed yourself up a little for the journey, and have made yourself ready. "For as the lightning cometh out of the east, and shineth even unto the west, so shall also the coming of the Son of man be." "For man also knoweth not his time; as the fishes that are taken in an evil net, and as the birds that are caught in the snare, so are the sons of men snared in an evil time, when it falleth suddenly upon them."

Then, what will death be to you, who are as yet all unprepared for a holy heaven, and for the holy society of God's great and glorious family which is assembled there in His august and holy presence, if you bestir not yourselves to take hold upon Jesus by faith, and to enter into covenant with God ere your feet stumble upon the dark and towering mountains of eternity, and your eyes close under the shades of the long, dreary, and starless night of the tomb. Death will come to you at Christ's appointed time—Christ has in His hand the key of the grave—but he will not come to take you home to glory. He will be to you Christ's executioner. He will come,—oh, dreadful thought!—to carry your poor, trembling, never-dying soul, down! down! down! for ever and for ever! into the lowest hell—for there *is* a hell of hells, as well as a heaven of heavens—and into the unbearable agonies there of unending perdition!

Are ye who read these lines not yet one with the Lord Jesus by faith, and safe in Him for eternity? Are ye yet out of the Ark of Ages, and is the deluge coming? Have you not yet fled to

Zoar, and is the torrent of burning displeasure from the presence of the Lord already beginning to flow in its smoking stream of hot indignation towards you to overwhelm and to scorch? Oh, flee to Jesus! He is the Munition of rocks! He is the only City of Refuge for eternity! In the view of the shipwrecked mariner, there is something in the life-boat, as it springs forward for his rescue to the place where he, lying tossed by the waves, is about to sink, that makes all the world nothing to him in comparison! In the view of the poor sick patient, there is a something about the physician that makes his presence the sunshine of comfort, and the very sound of his feet approaching his bed-side like the sweetest music upon his ear! The Lord Jesus is ready to become this to you. Oh, have ye not yet betaken yourselves to Him for salvation? Do you not yet believe in Him to the saving of your soul? Is the period of your sojourn on earth drawing to an end, and have you not yet begun to make preparation for eternity? I tell you, in Christ's name, who is able to save, and who is willing to become a Saviour even yet and even to you, that you have no time to lose, you have no time to trifle and to put off. I reverse the apostle's declaration when I thus address you. "The day is far spent, the night is at hand." The sun of your earthly existence is about to set. The shadows of *death's* dreary night are already beginning to descend loweringly upon your path; but what will death be to you who are out of Christ? Oh, it will be the thunder-bolt that is about suddenly to descend from the dark, overhanging, electric cloud of God's vengeance, to scorch, to crush, and to destroy that noble oak, with its branches spread to the four winds of heaven! It will be the terrific tornado that suddenly encircles the gallant vessel with its convulsive, whirling embrace, throwing it upon its beam-ends, and in a moment pushing it down and overwhelming it, in the foaming ocean's wide waste of waters! It will be the stone, unperceived by you, against which you in a thoughtless moment dash your foot whilst walking along the path that overhangs the rugged and frowning precipice, tripping you and hurling you headlong down into the horrible gulf below! Death to you will be the flight of hope from your bosom, and the enthronement of the fearful phantom of despair within the shrine of your desolated heart. It will be the extinguisher for ever of smiles that often before gleamed in their sunshine both upon your face and upon the countenances of those around you; for you will never smile after death, and even through all eternity you will never see a smile upon the sorrowful countenances of your companions in woe.

A WORD TO BELIEVERS.

Death to you is a very different event who are the children of God through faith in Christ Jesus. Your home at present is the house of God. Up from it you are to rise at death and enter heaven, your Father's home of love. You are now diligently preparing yourselves for the everlasting hereafter that awaits you, for you know that you are not to live in your present home of love for ever. Sad changes are awaiting you. A severance from all that is visible, and from the loved circle of your present friends, will sooner or later take place. Your last sickness will come. With a heart fainting and failing you will press your bed of affliction, from which you are not again to rise till lifted by the hand of friendship to be laid in the cold and dreary coffin. Verily there is much in death that is distressing to your fears, and blighting to your hopes, and painful to the tenderest sensibilities of your nature. The light of heaven's fair sun vanishing from your glazed and heavy eye; your heart ceasing to beat, standing still after many expansions and contractions, and remaining at rest like the pendulum of the clock when the owner omits to wind it up; the bosom ceasing to heave; the voices of your surrounding friends becoming more and more inaudible, and at last dying entirely away, like the receding notes of music whilst you are in the act of leaving the ball-room and departing home; the cold sweat standing in frigid drops upon your pallid brow; the restless tossing; the death struggle; the turning and the turning, the panting for breath; the look of anxiety upon those around for help; the wish to be up, and the recurring desire to get to bed again, but nowhere in your changed position can you obtain rest. This is trying; but hark! there is a voice from the throne that falls upon your ear, when the loving and long-familiar voices of friends around you in their sorrow become inaudible and die away, and which thus addresses you, "Fear not; I am the first and the last: I am he that liveth, and was dead; and, behold, I am alive for evermore, Amen; and have the keys of hell and of death." Heaven's high and joyful gates are flung open; angels are in your dying chamber; you have already bidden your friends adieu; you are entering upon the path that is to conduct you home. Death to you is your Redeemer's messenger; it takes you by the hand in the midst of your angel companions,—oh! the hand of the sable messenger is very cold, and you instinctively shrink from the touch,—and leads you up over a path that is overspread with a cloud resembling the pillar of cloud that followed the Israelites during their wilderness journeyings: one side, the side of nature, is dark,—the other side, the side of faith, the side turned to heaven, is light; that path ushers you into the living and peopled heavens and into Christ's unveiled and glorious presence; or rather, death is Christ himself come down to you in one or other of the troubles that are around you, that roam to and fro through the earth, and which are all His servants, that He may with a warm hand grasp yours, and lead you up and away from trouble and weakness to bask in the light of an unsetting sun, and in the enjoyment of an endless existence.

CHAPTER IX.

THE ENTRANCE OF GOD'S CHILDREN INTO HEAVEN.

CHRISTIANS generally, I believe, fail to realise in anything like an adequate manner what takes place when a child of God dies, rises from a bed of dissolution and enters into heaven. In truth, the entrance into heaven of another and another of God's redeemed and glorified children can scarcely be said to be realised by us at all. I appeal to your experience and to your recollections in confirmation of this assertion. You who have been in the chamber of bereavement, and have there seen a dear friend die, remember your views and feelings upon the occasion. How touching and impressive was to you what you saw! How dim and unrealised the great things which your faith, your creed, led you to believe were then transacting, but unseen by you!

You had, at the hour whilst standing beside your friend falling asleep in Jesus, a firm belief in the existence of heaven as the home to which God's dying children ascend,—in the continued existence of the soul in its state of separation from the body, —in the immediate entrance of the soul after death into the glories and joys of heaven; but with this belief, how dim, misty, and obscure were your views of what was taking place when your dying friend left you and rose to heaven. This, I believe, arises from two causes:—First, The soul, when departing, is not the object of sight to the bodily eye; second, Faith with us is weak. That faith which realises heaven as a great and existing world, and views the soul as still living when separated from the body by death, falls short of the vividness whereby we realise angels existing, or the Father and the Holy Spirit. Thus the *soul* of your friend rising, at the hour of death, from the midst of your family circle, surrounded by attending angels, its entrance into heaven, and joining God's children already there, are things around which, so far as you are concerned, there hangs a veil which your bodily eye cannot pierce, for what is transacting in the inside of that veil is entirely concealed from you.

In the chamber where we look on and see a dear friend die, we merely behold the change which death produces upon the body; and I am sure that I am speaking the experience of every mourner in Zion when I say, that the departure of the soul of a dear friend from the midst of us to enter heaven is not nearly so vividly realised as is the departure of a friend who leaves our home, and goes forth from the midst of us an emigrant to a foreign land.

In Elijah's translation to heaven you have a vivid picture of what takes place in your home when a dear friend, who is a child of God, leaves you at death, and enters into glory. Elijah receives intimation from God that the time of his departure from earth to heaven is at hand. He does what we should do in similar circumstances,—he sets his house in order, and takes an affectionate adieu with many friends whom he is leaving behind him. In the whirlwind, in the midst of a great company of angels, Elijah rises to heaven. But during his ascension, does he not look back and down upon earth, as the soul of your friend ascending to glory undoubtedly does, with fond and wistful eyes, like the emigrant in the vessel that is already under sail, who turns and gazes longingly upon the dear friends standing on the shore, and with their hats or handkerchiefs waving him a sorrowful adieu?

Again, you see the entrance of the soul of your friend into heaven, at the hour of departure, in Christ's ascension to glory. The Lord Jesus has ascended into heaven, our new covenant Head, our Forerunner into an eternity of bliss; and in His ascension you see what takes place when His people rise from their beds of death, and follow Him to the skies. View for a moment what takes place at your Redeemer's glorious ascension. He is among the living upon earth on the mount of Olivet. His disciples, in their sorrow at the thought of His going away, are around Him. Jesus is just about to leave them. "And when he had spoken these things, while they beheld, he was taken up; and a cloud received him out of their sight. And while they looked stedfastly toward heaven as he went up, behold, two men stood by them in white apparel; which also said, Ye men of Galilee, why stand ye gazing up into heaven? this same Jesus, which is taken up from you into heaven, shall so come in like manner as ye have seen him go into heaven." Angels in the sky, like a cloud of glory, escort the Son of God home to heaven. In Christ's ascension from the midst of His disciples gathered around Him, you see a vivid representation of what takes place when a beloved friend, at the hour of separation, rises from the midst of your assembled family circle and enters into heaven. It is thus every child of God is ushered into glory at death.

Enter with me the home of affliction, that you may see there how peacefully a believer can die, and hear from the lips of one who is now in bliss the hopes that gladdened her soul when the hour of her departure came:—"Oh! I have been happy here in the midst of my beloved family circle. I feel reluctant, my dear ones, to leave you, but my Father calls me home. I part with you, but I will meet you all again; for we have the good hope, through grace, that we are all now the members of the household of faith, and the heirs of eternal glory, and we will meet yonder, where friends part no more. 'O death, where is thy sting? O grave, where is thy victory? Thanks be to God, who giveth us the victory through Jesus Christ our Lord.' My dear partner, farewell! I have spent many happy years with you in this home of love. I will meet you again, not as a partner, but in the higher and sweeter and holier relation of a child of God, in yonder home of love, which our heavenly Father has already prepared for our reception. When we meet there, our troubles all past and left behind, death over, heaven entered, oh how happy for eternity will we be! I have walked with you in love, whilst you were all in all to me. I will meet you again, and walk with you again, in a better and holier world, and that through eternity, along the golden streets of the New Jerusalem! I have sat with you in the gladness of my heart, and have often talked with you in our home here about the comfort we felt in being able to look to God, now holding towards us the endearing relation of our Father in heaven; about Jesus, our Forerunner into a glorious eternity; about the Holy Spirit, by His work of grace upon our souls preparing us for glory; about heaven, as the home in which we are to dwell for ever; about angels and glorified saints, our companions for ever in the world of bliss. Yes, we will meet in yon happy world, and there, seated beneath the shade of the tree of life, with the river of life flowing in its limpid streams at our feet, we will talk again, not merely about what we *see, hear,* and *feel* in heaven, but—the faculty of memory remaining with us—about what we will experience after our separation, until we meet again. My beloved partner, farewell! Cheered by these high and heavenly hopes, remember me when I am gone, and diligently, assiduously, and prayerfully prepare to join me in God's unveiled presence above, whither I am going.

"My dear children, you cannot but weep; but sorrow not as those who have no hope. I am sorry to part with you, and especially as ye are yet but of tender age, little aware of the fickleness and deceitfulness of the world, and of the dangers that may await you in it. I could have wished, had it been our heavenly Father's will, to have acted as your guide for a few years longer, giving you my advice in seasons of perplexity and trial, and guiding you in the ways of the Lord. But, oh! my dear, dear children, you will soon be motherless! I know from my own young experience, what a sad thing it is to be deprived of a beloved mother's presence; but remember your Creator in the days of your youth. Live for God. Walk with Jesus in newness of life, love each other in the Spirit, prepare for glory; and oh! my dear children, when you leave successively your beds of death, and rise and follow me to heaven, I will meet you there, and will welcome you in, and will feel delighted to be with you all again in the same home of love. Dear friends all, farewell!"

She stops, unable to proceed. She speaks not again. She is done with the world. Her friends, in tears, look on, and behold the change which death produces in the countenance of that beloved partner and mother. A few heavy breathings follow. She clasps her hands as if engaged in secret prayer—she lifts her eyes to heaven, and taking one long, steady, penetrating gaze into the Holy of Holies, which she is just about to enter—she dies. This is all that is visible to the eye, and audible to the ear, in that chamber of dissolution; but how momentous are the events that then begin to be transacted on the other side of the veil! It is not difficult to realise that some of these, angels with the light of love upon their countenances, with the joy of heaven in their bosoms, and the glittering dew-drops of the morning of eternity upon their expanded wings, are in that chamber of death though unseen; they have been waiting like so many affectionate nurses for the birth of a child, till that child of God is ready to rise with them, and enter upon the path that is, in their company, to conduct her up to her rest. These angelic messengers see the patient dying, hear the expressions of affection she addresses to those around her, watch in sympathy the tears which the mourners around the dying bed are shedding. Patiently they wait till the emigrant to their own bright world is ready, till she enters the vessel of salvation, in which, along with them, she is to sail over the ocean of space that divides her home from heaven. At last the death-struggle with that dying saint is over; all is ready for her departure out of the midst of her sad family circle. The disembodied spirit is now free, able still to see and hear, and to communicate with other spirits. The angels are in motion; these bright visitors, again about to enter heaven, begin to rise. I cannot hear what communications they may make to that child of God as they ascend with her, and retrace the path along which they came when they left heaven upon their joyous mission. Assuredly the journey is not made in silence, no more than passengers in a ship are silent when crossing the ocean towards the haven on the other side, or acquaintances are in a railway train. That child of God, in the midst of her angel companions, rises higher and still higher upwards into the midst of the pure serene. What is she approaching? Heaven, Eternity, the great family of the bright and the blest. That home, as she rises upwards, bursts upon her view with its battlements of glory. It is a lovely dwelling. She sees the inmates looking forth from its doors of everlasting peace, and down upon her, whilst she is yet approaching them. How *lovely* appear their countenances! Beauteous is their form! Joyful is the sparkling expression of their eyes! How sweet is their voice when its silvery tones fall upon her ears! "Child of God! follower of the Lamb! we hail thy arrival upon this scene of love! Here is thy eternal home!"

CHAPTER X.

THE JOYFUL RECEPTION GIVEN TO THE CHILDREN OF GOD WHEN THEY RISE FROM EARTH AND ENTER HEAVEN.

IN this chapter I will endeavour to state and illustrate what *must* take place in heaven when a child of God rises from a bed of death upon earth and enters into glory. I do not found upon the three following *facts*, although they prove a glad reception to the redeemed when entering heaven,—that death to the believer is his birth into the family of God above, for he is then ushered into the world of glory; that the hour of death to the believer is his coronation season, when he rises from his previous state of minority, enters upon possession of the kingdom of glory, and receives from Christ the fulfilment of this promise, "Be thou faithful unto death, and I will give thee the tree of life;" that when the believer enters heaven he goes to the *marriage* supper of the Lamb, to have his spiritual espousals with Christ consummated, and publicly solemnised by the wedding guests who crowd the temple.

In proof of the joyful reception in heaven which the children of God who are there give to those entering it from earth, I point rather to these *two* other *facts*,—that *heaven is a home;* and that all who are in it, and all who go up to join them, constitute but *one family.* From these postulates I argue, I think logically, that when believers enter heaven at death, those already there must give them a joyful reception, a kind welcome home. It is natural to imagine this. It would be unnatural to suppose the contrary, *if* heaven be a home.

The Father, on the throne, sees in the entrance of every believer into glory, the fulfilment of His desire in that scheme of salvation which He devised in infinite mercy and originated in the high councils of heaven and in the sovereign deliberations of everlasting love. He loved that redeemed and now glorified one, even with an everlasting love; and surely it is not too much to suppose that He will, over that entrant from earth, rest in His love, rejoice over him with singing, and in calm joy receive him within the overshadowings of His infinite goodness. The Lord Jesus, on the right hand of the throne of God, sees in the entrance of every believer into heaven, evidence of the travail of His soul, and thus welcomes such home, "Come, ye blessed of my Father, inherit the kingdom prepared for you before the foundation of the world." The Holy Spirit sees, in every entrance of a believer into heaven, His own work of grace in his soul completed, and in joy receives him into His eternal peace.

How do angels usher or receive the redeemed into heaven? They shew their interest in the children of God by attending upon them and ministering to them *before* they enter; will angels lose their interest in God's children the moment they do enter? No! Angels will not leave those they have conducted home till they take them up to the throne, with glad hearts and joyful countenances, to present them to the Great Shepherd of Israel. It is only then they will feel that they have executed their mission. Single out in imagination, and thus try to realise the introduction of one child of God into heaven, encircled by her attending angels; the soul, say, of her whose death and entrance into heaven we attempted to portray in the end of the preceding chapter. May we not imagine the whole angels with their congratulations welcoming in the newly arrived from earth, whilst the immediate attending ones lead up the newly-glorified to the throne of God, and thus address Him who is upon it, "Father, Son, Holy Spirit, we bow to Thee! Thy glory is above the heavens; the earth is full of Thy praise. In obedience to Thy high command, we have visited the earth and have brought this beloved one home to glory. We feel glad, on her account, that her sufferings are over, and that now she is in heaven with us, free from pain and death, and in the enjoyment of eternal life. Sad was her parting in yon home of sorrow with her weeping friends, where her now sleeping body lies! but to the praise of Thy grace she was enabled, in tranquillity of mind and in serenity of spirit, to bear up under the separation. She has left a loving family in sorrow upon earth, and now we are glad to number her before Thee as a member of Thy great family who are here rejoicing around Thee. Her tears are all shed; her sorrows are all over; she will never feel again what it is to die. She is home in this world of life. We feel happy in the great happiness that awaits her here. To Thee, O God of salvation! and to the enfolding of Thy love, we deliver up our charge and commit this redeemed one. 'Salvation to him that sitteth upon the throne, and unto the Lamb, for ever and ever.' 'Worthy is the Lamb that was slain to receive power, and riches, and wisdom, and strength, and honour, and glory, and blessing.'"

Do not say that such a scene as I have described above cannot take place! Angels hovering upon their wings of light above the plains of Bethlehem, could thus address the trembling shepherds, "Behold, I bring you good tidings of great joy, which shall be unto all people." May they not then, when returning from earth into God's presence on high, say, "Behold, we have brought this blessed one home?"

The glorified who are in heaven feel a deep interest in the arrival of every member of the human family. And so they may; for they come to live with them for ever in the same home of love, to sing with them the same song, and to be their brethren in the Lord through eternity. When they meet yonder, they experience in the highest sense the unity of the spirit in the bond of peace; they see that they are truly one—all loved by the same Father, redeemed by the same Saviour, prepared for glory by the same Holy Spirit, one in the bundle of life. May we not most reasonably suppose, then, that those who are already in glory *will* give a welcome, refreshing, joyful, and gladdening, to those of their brethren from earth who enter, and join them where love in its purity reigns, and friendship in its truest glowings is felt?

"Brother! sister!" may those who are now in glory not exclaim, as another and another redeemed one from earth enters, "welcome home! Oh, what a portion awaits thee here! We never realised it in half its greatness whilst we were down in the world; the half was not told us yonder about it in the revelations of the Bible. See! what a bright heaven is around thee, illumined with the unveiled presence of God, and beaming with glory, filled with the light of a day to which no night comes, and crowded with inhabitants who never die. Behold yonder sun! the

Sun of righteousness that shines upon us never sets! The mountains of glory towering around in the verdure of an undecaying summer, and ascending not to the heavens but above them! we will climb them with thee, and shew thee from their tops of bliss the city of the living God, the heavenly Jerusalem, in whose golden streets throngs of joyous citizens pass and repass in their glory and beauty. Behold the valleys of delight, with the rivers of life meandering in their midst! we will walk with thee among their bowers of love, we will breathe with thee the balmy air of the heavenly paradise, we will sit with thee beneath the outspreading branches of the tree of life, and will tell thee what we have seen and experienced in this glad heaven. Come, thou blessed of the Lord! there is a long day before us, the day of eternal glory; beneath its shining we will shew thee the glories of heaven, its immortal curiosities. Come, we will feel its joys more ravishingly, shared in company with thee!"

Do you say that such a welcome as I have now portrayed cannot be given by the glorified to those from earth. I ask, Why not? Are the glorified in heaven, and their brethren from earth who enter and join them, not in the enjoyment of life and intelligence, having in full possession their reflective powers, whilst memory with them is not destroyed but strengthened? Are they not in possession of a social nature? Have they not the deepest and the tenderest sympathy towards each other as the members of the same family? Can they not speak to each other and give expression to their sympathy? Are they not in heaven exactly what they were in a state of grace upon earth, only perfected? I venture to assert that the members of God's family who are in heaven *must* be far more changed than I believe them to be, if they give not a reception to those joining them even more enthusiastic than I have depicted.

A welcome is given to those returning to their native land when entering the home of their friends upon earth. Look in with me upon yonder family circle. The father has been absent for years in a foreign land; but, whilst at a distance, his family did not forget him. Often its members talked about him, frequently they wrote letters to him whilst away; they received letters in return from him. Now that father is on his way home; the day of his arrival is known. This is the day. That home is now in all the bustle of a fond expectation. The carriage is sent to the train to convey him. It is already at the gate, with a beloved father in it! Describe to me, if you can, the fondness, the joyfulness of the reception which the family give him when the carriage stops at the door! The fond partner meets her beloved with a glow in her bosom of a love which absence, instead of cooling, has the more inflamed. The children scream with the outburst of childish delight, and rush into their father's opened arms. All there are in a commotion of bewildered joy; a thrilling gladness streams through every bosom over the long-absent one's return. Indeed, that home would not be a home of love,—as heaven is,—if a welcome, such as I have described, were not given to him who thus returns and joins his family circle.

Take an example from yon crowded railway-station! Among those assembled there you witness two brothers and two sisters, in a state of excitement and gladness, waiting the arrival of the train. A younger sister has been for years absent from her home, and now she is on her way back. When the train stops, and the passengers emerge from its compartments, and their young sister appears and bursts upon their view with the smile of recognition upon her countenance, her brothers and sisters clasp her by the hand, kiss her, and give her the most kindly welcome home.

Or behold yon anxious mother standing upon the quay, among the crowd around her, waiting there the arrival of the steam-boat that is now not far off: she has an only son on board who has been abroad for a season, and he is coming to see her and to stay with her in her home. When the boat arrives, how eagerly she rushes forward, clasps her dear one in her arms, and pours upon him all the warm gushing fondness of a mother's welcome the moment he steps on shore.

There is a ship upon the bosom of the Mediterranean Sea! The season when it should be gliding there with its outspread sails is past, and sailing is now dangerous. The apostle Paul is in it, and along with him there are two hundred and seventy-five souls. The clouds are moving in the sky with that sable, heavy, and lowering aspect which betoken the approach of the storm; a murky gloom is brooding around upon the waters. At last the storm in its fury rises; the winds begin to blow with terrific gusts; the sea is moved into billows mountains high; a darkness that is felt comes down upon the deep; neither sun nor stars for many days appear; all hope is taken away that those on board can be saved. In this extremity an angel from the court of heaven is sent down by Him who is upon the throne, to intimate to the apostle Paul that all the passengers will be saved, but the ship is to be wrecked and lost. The ship accordingly is driven onwards by the storm, and is stranded upon the shore of the island of Melita; there it goes to pieces. The passengers, however, are saved—some on boards, and some on broken pieces of the ship; and so it came to pass that they all escaped safe to land. The sacred historian thus describes the reception which those thus saved receive from the inhabitants who meet them on the shore:—"And when they were escaped, then they knew that the island was called Melita. And the barbarous people shewed us no little kindness: for they kindled a fire, and received us every one, because of the present rain, and because of the cold."

Is this the reception given to the shipwrecked passengers upon *that* shore? And will any one venture to tell me that when *you*, a child of God, shall suffer shipwreck by death upon the shore of mortality, leave your body, like a vessel stranded and motionless upon the beach, rise to heaven, enter it, and join God's children who are living there, that the inhabitants of heaven will give you a colder reception upon the shores of Immanuel's land than these islanders did to Paul and to his fellow-passengers? No, it cannot be! The whole of the glorified from earth who are yonder, except two, have been encompassed by the storm of sickness, and have suffered the shipwreck of death. Having thus passed through the floods before you, when they meet you, or rather when you meet them, on yon bright shore, they will shew you no little kindness, and give you a reception joyful and ardent, as they unitedly and exultingly welcome you home.

CHAPTER XI.

THE JOY OF ONCE SEPARATED FRIENDS MEETING IN HEAVEN—THE WORLD OF REUNIONS.

THE meeting of dear friends, even upon earth, who have been separated for a season, is an occasion of joy. I do not require to enter into any lengthened illustration of this. You who read have felt this often in your own past experience. A separation for a season—whether forced or voluntary—from friends you love, awakens a higher tide of joy in your bosom when you meet than you could have felt had no separation taken place.

The same is true respecting dear friends who meet in heaven, their Father's home, after a separation for a season effected by death. The hour of parting in the chamber of dissolution is a season of sorrow, at least to the friends who are left in their bereavement, if not also to the departing saint who rises from the midst of them to enter *heaven.* The reunion of these dear friends in heaven, beyond death and the grave, *must* necessarily be a meeting of joy.

I believe that Christians generally, in the season of bereavement, have done a great injury to their feelings and longings, and have deadened sadly their immortal hopes, by imagining that they are to be totally different in their social feelings towards their friends when they meet in heaven from what they were here. They will be different, but simply in the sense that they will be perfected in everything, their friendships included. The sainted child will meet the sainted mother in heaven; and looking at their meeting in the light of the doctrine that there is in a state of glory the recognition of friends, their reunion *must* be a source of joy.

Do not tell me that my mother will no longer be my mother when I rise and meet her in heaven. I do not understand such language. When I rise to heaven, and meet the being there who *was* my mother, and when I look upon her, and speak with her in the language God's children use above, I *may* not call her mother up yonder; but as I point to her, and speak about her to some kindred saint or accompanying angel, will I say, There is the being who *was* my mother, or, There *is* my mother? I do not see that it is in the power even of omnipotence to extinguish the *fact*, that when I meet my mother in heaven, I am in the presence of the being who gave me birth, except by extinguishing her or me. Carrying this fact along with us, in its application to others of our present relative unions, I address myself to you who, in the providence of God, may be mourning in Zion over the departure of a friend dear and fondly beloved.

I address you who mourn the loss of a beloved mother. Are you now cherishing many fond and tender recollections about what she was, and about what she was to you? In your remembrance of her, was she all that was lovely, all that was holy, all that was heavenly and pure, whilst she yet remained with you in your home? Did you feel your young heart touched with the many nameless manifestations of her maternal regard for you? and did your soul glow back again towards her with all the warm emotions of a responsive affection? Was her voice like the music of heaven to your ear; her smile, so seldom absent from her countenance, the sunshine of your purest comfort upon earth; the lustred expression of her eye, like the bursting forth upon you of a warm summer's morning, whilst the earth is all in a glitter around with its dew-drops sparkling in their beauteous robes, and smiling in their responsive love to the rising sun? Was her presence in your home like an unsetting sun shining upon you from a firmament of love?

Is this bright scene, with which you were once encircled, now, alas! changed? Has a winter of desolation spread itself suddenly, with its howling winds and its piercing cold and its snows and its sleet, over your now desolated and sorrowing heart? Has the loneliness of a sore bereavement descended upon your emptied home? Is your mother a stranger now in your house, which she once so much adorned? Oh! every look you take back with the eye of memory upon these scenes of pure domestic endearments makes your present desolation the more sad.

In your fond recollections you see your beloved mother as if still lying, resigned, yet hopeful, upon that bed where she yielded up her redeemed and regenerated spirit to God, and where she felt the gracious presence of Jesus overshadowing her, and filling her fainting soul with the breathings of His love and the rich consolations of His grace. That chamber was to her the house of God and the very gate of heaven, the gateway through which she was about to pass into the unveiled presence of Him whom she so ardently loved, the painful avenue that was to conduct her to eternal glory. Do you still hear her, at least are her words still echoing through the chambers of memory, speaking about the happy land and the lovelier home she was so soon to enter, the holier voices and the sweeter songs of praise which she was so soon to hear rising around her in the heaven of heavens? Do you seem still to hear her voice, tremulous with the commingled emotions of sorrow, and of love, and of holy hope, bidding you a solemn, an affecting, a soul-thrilling farewell? And do you even yet seem to feel the spasmodic pressure of her fevered and trembling hand, as she looked up with the light of heaven upon her pale countenance, the beamings of divine love and of holy hope in her dying eye, and said, "The Lord bless you and keep you, my dearly beloved child. I am going home to *my* Father and *your* Father, to *my* God and *your* God. Oh! I feel it sad to part with thee, my beloved one; but our separation will not be long! Live above the world: live for God. Entrust your all to Jesus; walk in the Spirit; prepare daily and diligently to meet me in yonder joyous heaven. And then, oh! my dear child, when you are like me now, ready to be offered, and the time of your departure is at hand, and when you rise from the clouds and the gloom of the dark night of death to the bright realms of eternal day, I will be the first to meet you at the gate of heaven, and to welcome you in to take your place beside me in our Father's happy home."

Do you still seem to see before you the calm yet penetrating look of that eye, just closing upon all the visibilities of time, when the spirit was hovering upon the very verge of the boundless provinces of eternity, and looking in with a scrutinising gaze upon the awful profound beyond,—looking down, as it were, from the quay upon the vessel lying afloat in the harbour, in which she was to embark and sail over the mysterious ocean, on the other side of which a harbour was opening its peaceful bosom to receive the vessel, amid the light of eternal day, and amid the acclamations of millions of millions who were ready to welcome the emigrant to join them in the better land. Do you see your mother still in her departure from you, whilst standing in her death-chamber, not only embarking, but in imagination do you see the sails of the vessel yet outspread, and becoming gradually less and less, on the verge of the far-off ocean, until you beheld her on the other side entering a haven of rest for ever on yon peaceful shore, which no storm with its rolling billows ever lashed, and over whose landscapes of loveliness and beauty no hurricane of wind ever passed. You will meet with many whom you knew upon earth, who were your friends and acquaintances and companions here; but oh,—joyful thought!—you will meet your mother also in heaven. Image your departure from this world come, you ascend upwards and yet upwards towards your Father's home. The cry arises from your angelic attendants around you, exultant and rejoicing: "Lift up your heads, O ye gates, even lift them up, ye everlasting doors, that this other child of God and heir of glory may come in." Your mother gave you the promise upon her death-bed that she would be upon the confines of the realms of bliss, would wait for your arrival there, and would be the first to welcome you into your Father's home. Lo! yonder she stands in her robe of white. Many are looking forth from the shores of immortality upon you rising to heaven. Do you see yon shining and resplendent child of God, with the robe of white so glistening, the crown so sparkling, the glow of heavenly love so radiant in the sleepless eye, standing on the very front rank of the congregated assemblies of heaven, who are about to welcome you to the sky? That is your mother. She knows you are coming; she remembers her parting promise in her chamber of dissolution; she remembers the sorrow you mutually felt when she left you. There she is, waiting for your uprising; and oh, how ardently she is longing to meet you! You reach the outskirts of the realms of eternal day; you land; your mother springs forward to be the first to receive you; she clasps you to her glorified bosom; she welcomes you home; your parting with her in the world below was sorrowful. Oh, how joyful will you be when you thus meet in your Father's home above, never to part again whilst the glad cycles of a smiling eternity are rolling over you!

Again, I address you who have been parted by death from a venerable father—a father whom you loved in the Lord. Do you remember the time, when, morning and evening, you felt your heart thrilled by the deeply emotional tones of his voice, whilst as a family you knelt in prayer before God's throne of grace? Do you still see, as it were, in imagination, the pious group of your family circle, with your father acting as its high priest, kneeling in lowly adoration before your God? Do you still, as it were, hear your father's voice in his conversations with you, reminding you that he had lived the threescore years and ten which God by the fiat of His sovereignty has allotted to man upon the earth, and that, during that whole period, he had been witnessing one star after another shooting off from the firmament of life and descending into the dark night of the grave? Do you remember him telling you with the deepest emotion how this view of a changing past led him to look up for a home, not upon earth, and to speak to you with the rapturous glow of a heavenly hope about the home which he knew his dear Redeemer was preparing for him and for you in heaven? Whilst you listened to your father's loving voice, speaking to you about the rest which remains for the people of God, did you feel as if eternity had descended, had moved towards you, unbosoming to your view its great realities, and as if heaven had come near? Did you feel that your dear father had reached its threshold, where he was about to bid you adieu for a short season, to walk in, to look upon its glories, to share its joys, and to mingle with its gladdened assemblies? Is your father now gone? Has he left you to walk in your sorrow without him in this vale of tears? Did you see him sicken? Did you see him die? Did you see him, as if in a calm and peaceful sleep—a lake with its bosom all placid and calm and unruffled by even one stir of the gently sighing breeze—fall asleep in Jesus, pass away, and leave you in all the loneliness and in all the dreary desolation of a sore bereavement? Do you still see pictured in the chamber of memory the large and respectable company, who, in their sable robes and in the hush of a heavy silence, met in your home on your dear father's funeral day? Do you see the attendants still, as it were, in the act of bearing the coffin out from the dear old home he was leaving for ever—the coffin in which his cold remains lay asleep? Do you still see, as it were, the hearse with its nodding plumes moving off from a desolate dwelling—your father going to his long home, and the sorrowful mourners following? Do you still, in imagination, stand at that newly-opened grave, which had been prepared to receive in charge, till the resurrection morning dawns, the sacred deposit of your father's ashes, and look at the coffin for the last time, when the cords were let go, as if the cable had been cut, and the vessel let loose to sail away upon the waters of a dull and motionless sea? Did you then lift your hat, not merely to bid farewell, a long farewell, to the sleeping dead, but to raise your soul, whilst uncovered, in a short prayer to your Father in heaven, and to commit yourself in your season of bereavement to the sleepless watchfulness and care and omnipotent guardianship of your covenant-keeping God, even to Him who never changes and who never dies? Did you bow to the funeral attendants just before their dispersion, as they stood with saddened countenances around the new filled-up grave, in token of your grateful appreciation of their sympathy and attendance, whilst the cold, cold sod above your father's breast was marking the place where the dear one lay? Did you then turn your back on that grave, and return with a sad and desolated heart to the lonely home from which your father had been removed, and from which he was gone for ever? Oh! when you enter amid the silence of this bereavement, and look upon the empty chair in which he so long and so venerably sat, and see in every object that meets your eye a witness that tells you your father is not here,—you are even then not without hope. Is your name in the Book of Life? Are you walking in the footsteps of the dear departed one? Are you, as he was, followers of God as dear children. Are you, as he did whilst in life, walking in love, as Christ also loved you, and gave Himself for you an offering and a sacrifice to God for a sweet smelling-savour? Are you living in the Spirit, and thus preparing for the world of glory which your father has entered? Do you still remember him, now that he is in heaven? Are you anxiously longing to be where he is?

Are you diligently preparing to join him in your Father's house above, there to see his face, to hear his voice, and to walk with him in love through the courts of glory? Your present preparation for heaven will not be in vain, and your earnest yearnings to be with your father in glory God will ere long fulfil. Yet a little while, and you will leave your present earthly home. Prepared and ready, you will enter your sick chamber and lie down upon your bed of dissolution. Image the hour come. With your heart and flesh fainting and failing, you are leaving the earth; but it is to rise to heaven. You are leaving time; but it is to rise and enter a glorious eternity. You are leaving dear friends, weeping children, who are looking with sorrowful hearts and tear-bedimmed countenances upon you—now a father too—whilst bidding them adieu; but you are about to enter a glad eternity, there to meet, not merely your heavenly Father, Jesus, the Holy Spirit, angels and glorified saints, but him a saint also whom you once called father upon earth, and who, so far as I can see, you may with perfect propriety call father when you rise and meet him in heaven.

When Elijah rose in the whirlwind to heaven, Elisha beheld him, and exclaimed, "My father! my father!" When you rise to heaven at death, and meet your father in its glad and rejoicing home—oh! as you recognise him in the light of a glorious eternity, and remember his sorrowful parting from you in his chamber of dissolution,—will ye not in an ecstacy of joy rush into his arms as he advances to meet you, and whilst he embraces you, will ye not involuntarily and joyously exclaim, "My father! my father!"

CHAPTER XII.

THE JOY OF FRIENDS MEETING IN HEAVEN—(*continued.*)

AGAIN, I address you who have, in the providence of God, lost a lovely, a beautiful, a fondly-beloved daughter. Is your memory still floating upon the past, like the thoughts of a sleeper at night upon the visions of the bright day that is gone? Are you gazing still upon her opening beauties with all the partial fondness of a loving parent's heart? Do you see her a helpless babe, with the smile of the cherub upon her little, sweet, enchanting, and lovely face? Do you see her still, as it were, nestled as of yore in the trust and in the confidence of an appropriating faith upon your fond and gladdened breast? Did you see her grow up from infancy to girlhood, with her bright blue laughing eyes, with her cheeks vying to outblush the tinge of the opening rose when dipped in the dew of the morning, with her golden hair in graceful ringlets parted and clustering over her marble brow and dangling in many a graceful curl round about her ivory neck? Did you see the laughing, romping, fawn-like girl expand before you in loveliness like the opening rose, and at last bloom into the blush and graceful timidity of the highly-accomplished, serene-countenanced, and sensitively-refined young lady? Did you feel your heart dance at the sound of her voice, soft and sweet in *your* ear, like the tones of the Æolian harp? Did you feel your bosom glow more and more in love to her as you looked upon her opening beauties expanding before you, and as you felt that your love to her was met and returned by the responsive glow of the tenderest filial affection in all its unaffectedness and purity? Did you see this fair summer-scene in your sweet home of love suddenly changed? Did you see the bright blue sky overcast, and the heavens above you begin to lower?—her sun go down whilst it was yet day? Did you see the dark clouds of affliction, like melancholy tidings casting their shadows before them, begin to gather and hover heavily over your home?—a beloved daughter's countenance changed? Did you see that eye that beamed upon you for years with an intelligent mildness, like a calm blue lake encircled by roses, and breathed upon by the fragrant breezes of heaven, close before you in the cold, upturned, and fixed gaze of death?—the lips change in their colour from the hue of the cherry into the livid expression of a shrivelled and wasted grape? Did you see her laid out, cold, motionless, and decayed, like a faded, withered lily encircled by a wreath of snow beneath the white drapery of the winding-sheet? Is that once beloved one,—the light of your eye, the joy of your heart, the richest gem in your crown of family happiness,—still before you in the visions of the night, and in the meditations of the day, the very memory of whom is like a gleam of light and of comfort upon your now darkened and benighted path?

Image the feeling of that ascended and glorified daughter, when her mother also ascends from *her* death-bed and meets her again. And what are the anticipations of that glorified mother as she rises beneath the opening heavens with the hope of meeting her dearly-beloved one in the enjoyment of her eternal rest? She is exulting and glad in the great thought that soon she will see the ineffable glory and enjoy its life,—that there she will see God unveiled; Jesus, in the Father's very image, at the right hand of the throne of the Majesty in the heavens; the Holy Spirit, the fountain of life in heaven and all its joys; angels and glorified saints, in their inconceivable numbers and radiant forms. But, oh! there is one, a sacred one, a dear one, she has in view as she rises and approaches nearer and still nearer, one she longs and pants to meet,—it is her daughter, who left her so lovingly in her death-chamber to enter before her into glory.

The mother rises, she enters, she pauses within the veil, she looks around her, and, lo! what a sight! Heaven has burst upon her view, the throne of God, and Him unveiled who is upon it. She sees around her prodigious assemblages of living angels and saints. She meets friends who had gone before her to the happy land. But more exquisitely ravishing still to her glorified soul,—fond, and longing for the reunion,—she meets her daughter! Yes! her own, her beloved daughter! And now there is in her countenance no trace of the ravages of disease, and in her eye there is not now the dimness and languor of death! Their parting was sorrowful in their home upon earth, but joyful is their meeting up yonder in heaven, their Father's home! They meet in gladness, never to part.

Again, I address you who now mourn the loss of a beloved partner. Have you, like Abraham, been called upon, with your bosom flooded by the tides of a bitter sorrow, to rise up in your tears and to bury your dead out of your sight? Were you lovely in your lives? Did you, like Zacharias and Elizabeth, walk hand in hand in all the commandments and in all the ordinances of the Lord blameless? In your union, and in the unceasing and nameless reciprocations of affection betwixt you, did you see Christ's covenant-union with your souls shadowed forth, and His endearments and heavenly breathings of love bestowed upon you both typified? Did you feel, as it were, a new sun in your sky, and the brilliancy of an unclouded sunshine falling upon your path, as she walked in her beauty along with you in the covenant of your God? Did you feel the dawning around you of a morning that shone brighter and brighter till it passed into the cloudless day of unsullied joy, when she arose in her loveliness upon your path, and when she brought summer to your soul, with its light and warmth, by her smile? Do you still see, as it were, through your present tears, that countenance upon which you never even once beheld a frown, as a vapour bedimming the bright blue sky? Do you still seem to behold these eyes beaming forth upon you, like two morning-stars shining from the sky that is overhanging you like a cloudless ocean of serenity? Do you see her still flitting to and fro through the chambers of your memory, like Beauty's own impersonation walking among the Graces in the bowers of happiness? Is this season of sunshine and of joy that was once yours now a thing of the past? Has your bright day of former comfort now closed amid the gathering darkness of a night of sorrow? Has a night of clouds and of darkness gathered over you and settled down upon your desolated heart? Is the once dearly-beloved one away—the light of your soul gone? Did you see her leave you in your sorrow and embark upon a dark and stormy ocean to cross over to yon world on the other side, where the inhabitant never says, "I am sick," where the tear of separation was never shed, where the sigh of bereavement was never heard, and where the pang of parting was never felt—and where you will again meet her, on the brightening morning of your entrace into a glorious eternity, and feel gladdened when you again join her in your Father's home, and behold her so much fresher and fairer and so much more blooming and beauteous than ever you saw her upon earth, lovely to your eye though she was whilst here? And when you meet her up *yonder* you will recognise her, and again walk with her as in former days—not as a partner, but as a child of God—by the sequestered vale of eternal blessedness, and sit beside her upon the mountain-side of everlasting joy, and you will there tell her, in the language of heaven, how lonely you felt in the earth below and in your home of bereavement after you were parted from her at the sorrowful hour of her death.

Is she away? Has she vanished like a bright apparition of joy into the silence and darkness of the grave, who was once like a sunbeam of light and of comfort upon your path and in your home? And as you sit in your desolated dwelling, does memory conjure up bright visions of former joys in connexion with her that is gone, that are now, alas! alas! merely numbered among the things that were? Do you remember, in your present desolation, the time when you first met her in the intercourse of life,—when you first felt your heart enthralled by the music of her voice, and when you first began, with an opening perception and with a responsive thrill of affection, to see in *her* countenance what you never saw in another. Do you remember the day of your youthful espousals—the day of the gladness of your hearts—the happy evening when, in the midst of the gathered assemblage of friends and acquaintances, she became yours?—when, beneath the blazing light of the bright chandelier, you saw her, followed by her bridesmaids dressed in white and with wreaths upon their brows, advance blushing in her maiden modesty to the place where you stood? Then came the thrill of an almost unbearable emotion that went to your very heart when at the bidding of the man of God she laid her hand in yours, when you pressed it gently in a tremor of delight, when you listened with an almost choking emotion of gladness to the official declaration that you had become *one*. How happily you lived with her in your married state, and how gladsomely your days were spent in her company. Are these days and are these scenes past, never again to return? Has that loved one left you, and passed away for ever? Is she now the cold inmate of yon cold grave where you laid her deep in the slumber of death, and where yon left her in her sleep? You have reared a monument to her memory, and carved the inscription upon it that tells, in the words of affection, how dear she was to you whilst she lived, and how hallowed her memory is in your fond remembrance still, now that she is dead? Did she fall asleep in Jesus, and leave you at her death expressing to you her fond hope and longing desire of meeting you at last in heaven, your Father's home? If you are also a child of God and an heir of glory, your separation will not be long. When away from your home for a season, whilst she yet lived with you in your bower of love upon earth, how proudly, how joyously did she welcome you in at your return, with the smile of true affection upon her face, and the flutter of delight in her bosom! Even thus will she welcome you up into heaven, to meet her there, and to dwell again with her there, when the hour of your departure is come, —when you rise in the chariot of salvation, and receive from her yonder a welcome, warmer and more joyous than was ever given, in the outburst of conjugal affection, to the returning upon earth.

I now address you who mourn the loss of a beloved husband, and who are feeling sorrowfully the change which his removal from you has effected in your home. Did he walk with you in love whilst here, his conversation in heaven, his heart there, and with many aspirations after the heavenly glory? The trouble at last came, whilst walking thus together in love and in the covenant of your God, that laid him low before you on his bed of sickness? Like Martha and Mary in their home of sorrow, did you watch with a sad and bewildered heart the setting of the sun of his earthly existence, and the gradually gathering gloom around the bed of the sinking invalid of the dreary night of the grave? By the appearance of the changing countenance, it was too sure that your separation from the beloved one was approaching, and would soon be effected. The last night thus came. You could not leave him; you could not go to bed; you could not trust the hand of another to minister to him those cordials which the promptings of affection so instinctively suggest, and the hand of love so softly and gently administers. The night passed heavily over you; the very sound of the wind without seemed the sigh of nature's sympathy with you in your sorrow and gathering desolation. At last the light of the returning morning began to break in the east, and a sleeping world was about to awake to life and activity; whilst—oh, sad change! —your beloved partner was about to close his eyes in the sleep of the grave. Feeling his departure near, did he take you by the hand, look pensively into your face, and bid you a fond, faltering, lingering farewell? Almost unable to speak, did he whisper to you in his last breathings, his continued trust in his Saviour, his hope of a blessed immortality? Did he look up, with the radiancy and gleamings of a holy joy upon his pallid countenance, whilst he asked you not to sorrow; for you, as a child of God, would yet rise and meet him in heaven, and spend a glorious eternity with him there? Whilst the increasing light of the morning's sun was pouring its returning tides of life and gladness upon a living world, did your dear husband leave you, fall asleep in Jesus, rise upwards to glory, enter the realms of eternal day, and find himself home with God? He is not now in your home, so changed in its aspect, so sad in its gloom; but he lives still; he is in the world of life above—an inmate of heaven—a member of God's great and happy family there, whose time of weeping is over. He is not now in your company; his words of love, to which he is still giving utterance, are not falling upon your ear; but look up in hope; he is among the redeemed who stand in white before the throne of God; he is mingling with their assemblies, and often and fondly may he now be speaking to some dear friend of yours and of his, whom he has met above, of the joy he will feel when you too rise at your death, and meet him in glory—when he will hear your voice, your well-known voice again, and see your face amid the light of a glorious eternity, beaming upon him, as of yore, in its joy and friendship, in a home where love never cools, lovers never part, and where friends meet to be together for ever.

Mourner in Zion! image the hour when you will leave your sorrows here and follow the dear one to the skies! Your friends are gathered in their sympathy around your dying bed. Angels are receiving the command from God to go down and conduct you home. They are leaving for a little the presence of your now glorified partner, who is still dear to you, and fond about you still as a sister in the Lord ; with him these angels have previously been associating in all the freedom of love and intercourse that exist among the members of the whole of God's family in heaven ; he has heard them receive the command from God to descend to your sick-chamber, that they may convey you up to meet him, and see him, and speak with him again. Whilst they are absent on their mission, will your dear partner feel no anxiety about their return, and no interest about the moment when your entrance into heaven will take place? Assuredly he will. Assuredly, with the fond, longing, reiterated look of one who is expecting the coming of some dear one to a home here, he will fondly gaze upon the path by which he beheld your angelic guides descend, and along which they will again return, when they rise with you to the world above. When he sees these angelic messengers, like a moving white cloud, emerge into his view from the great abyss of space below ; and beholds you, in the midst of them, burst upon his view, clothed in the white robe of your Redeemer's imputed righteousness, lovely as an angel of God, his soul will glow and quiver with a tremor of delight, and more intense will be his emotions when he meets you on the threshold, and welcomes you home to heaven, to be with him through eternity in the same home. The joy of this meeting will efface, at once and for ever, the sorrow which his sad departure from you awakened in your soul. Child of God! sorrow not in thy present bereavement, as those who have no hope. Thou hast not only the hope of heaven, as a home thou art yet to enter, leaving the sorrows of earth behind; thou hast also the hope—the very sunshine of joy upon thy present dark path—of meeting, in realms of love and of life, him who is gone before, who is, like thy Saviour, remembering thee in the skies, and is longing, with all the fondness of an unquenchable love, for the time when thou wilt rise from earth and join him in his joy—a joy death will never extinguish again, and no after parting will ever diminish.

CHAPTER XIII.

ELEMENTS OF JOY TO FRIENDS MEETING IN HEAVEN.

THERE are many elements of joy which the children of God possess when they meet in heaven. The beatific vision, the sight of the face of God, which makes happy; full, free, and endearing personal intercourse with Jesus; the visibly unfolded presence of the Holy Spirit as He moves upon their souls in His breathings of life and of love; the companionship of angels; free and loving intercourse with their fellow-saints; heaven their glorious and blissful home for eternity; sin, death, separation, and all other causes of sorrow, removed from them; all the fountains of God's own joys open to them;—these are elements of comfort to those meeting in heaven, which are obvious to every Christian, and need no illustration. Instead of dwelling upon these, I will rather advert to some other elements of joy which the children of God possess when they meet in heaven, which have not been much dwelt upon by religious writers, but which, when properly viewed, will, or at least ought, to exert a very great influence upon our views and conduct here.

The glorified in heaven are in full possession of their memory; this is to them an element of joy.

Memory will open to you a wide fountain of joy who are now separated from dear friends fallen asleep in Jesus, when you rise at your death and meet them in heaven. The very remembrance yonder of your separations from them for a season, of the days and years you spent in thinking of their loss; the longing wishes that often rose in your sorrowful bosom, that you might rise and meet them in heaven, and see them again, and speak to them again; the power of identifying them, when you rise and meet them, as the very friends who loved you so fondly, and felt for you so deeply, whilst they remained with you in your home upon earth; these separations from them over, this will be an element of joy to your souls when you meet them again. With what fondness, with what joy and delight will you meet your mother, your father, your partner, your children, your brothers, your sisters, your many other friends, who were dear to you on earth, with the recollection of your sad separation for a season, and with the knowledge that another parting will never occur! How joyful will it be for you to say when you meet them, "Thank God, we will never be parted again!"

The glorified meet in heaven in possession of their social affections; this is another element of joy.

Not merely will all the intellectual faculties of our souls remain with us up in heaven—our understanding and judgment, by which we will distinguish our former friends who are with us before the throne of God from other saints who are associating with us there—our memory, which will bring up to us, in connexion with the dear and beloved ones, the whole day of our intercourse with them below, that was so suddenly and so sadly succeeded by the dark night of bereavement caused by their death;—our *social affections* will remain when we enter heaven; and this will be to us, in our intercourse with our friends above, an open and a constantly flowing fountain of joy.

We have social affections here; and this fact affords the presumption that we will possess the same up in heaven. The Lord Jesus is the same yesterday, to-day, and for ever. He shewed whilst upon earth that He was in possession of all the social affections of our nature, and that without sin. He is the same still. He sits upon the throne, with a bosom glowing towards all the inhabitants of heaven, and towards all the children of men upon earth, with all the warmth of the loves and sympathies of our moral nature.

With what delight will you meet your dear friends in heaven, you and they in possession still of these sympathies! You will not meet merely with perfect intellects, with souls capable of enjoying divine delights in communion with Father, Son, and Holy Spirit; you will, through the retention of your social affections, have souls capable of enjoying to the full the company of those friends in heaven who spent with you their short day of life upon earth, with whom you took sweet counsel in the world below, went up to the house of God in company, often kneeled together at a throne of grace, and sung with delight as with one voice the praises of your God.

Some of the relationships in which we now stand to each other will not remain in heaven; many of them will not be needed there. I believe, however, that our Christian companionships and friendships formed here will, or at least *may*, be resumed and perpetuated there. Our social affections will be the foundation upon which these perpetuated friendships will rest. Will I be able to love my mother when I meet her in heaven? I believe I will. No doubt God, Jesus, the Holy Spirit, will be supremely loved by me when I stand before the throne of God; but when I meet my mother there, I will assuredly single her out from the rest of the glorified saints who are round about the throne, walk with her in her robe of white, love her in the Lord as I did upon earth, but much more purely and warmly, continue through eternity in heaven the companionship of Christian love which had its origin with us in the providential arrangements of the God of our salvation. How joyous will eternity be, thus spent not only in communion with God and in His praise, but in high and social companionship with those whom we loved upon earth!

The glorified in heaven possess the full recognition of their friends; this is another element of joy.

I have endeavoured in "Heaven our Home" to *prove* that we will recognise our friends when we rise and meet them in heaven. I only wish here to remind my reader that this recognition will be an element of joy to us, when we rise and meet them above.

Recognition will be an element of sorrow, of additional agony, to the lost in hell. Let the wicked in their present ungodly companionships bear this in remembrance. What will you feel when you meet and recognise in the place of despair one whom you led on to ruin whilst upon earth? Will such a recognition not add immensely to your torment there?

At the risk of some repetition of a theme glanced at in a prior volume, I address you who may be guilty before God of the fearful sin of seduction. You deliberately planned and ultimately effected the ruin of one whose chief guilt in sinning with you was, that she loved you too fondly, and confided in you too much. You left her after you ruined her, to reap the harvest of shame brought upon her by your misconduct. Alas! she was unable to bear her disgrace or retrieve her fall. In an evil hour she fled from her parents' home, who, bitterly and with many tears, lamented the untimely withering of their cherished flower, and that through you. She thoughtlessly, alas! and recklessly betook herself to the haunts of iniquity, that she might smother there the upbraidings of conscience in the cup of intoxication, in the song of licentiousness, in company with those who have flung off the fear of God, and who live in the world unmindful of the great futurity before them. Alas! the Scriptures announce a terrible truth when they say, "The way of transgressors is hard." The girl you ruined finds it so; her constitution speedily gives way, she is laid upon a bed of disease, forsaken by her companions in guilt, away from her mother's attentions and her father's care; she dies impenitent, and goes down into an eternity of woe. You, her seducer, have caused all this ruin. She was well brought up, she had the example of a living Christianity set before her in her parents' lives; she listened every morning and evening in her girlhood to the affectionate prayers of her beloved father, poured out before God in her behalf from the fulness of a loving heart, that the Great Shepherd would enfold in His everlasting arms this lamb of the flock; the blossoms of early piety appeared thick upon her in the morning of life; but *you*, her vile seducer, withered them and ruined her. Image your feelings when you—if you also die impenitent—meet her in the lake of woe. As she turns upon you, her eye flashing fire amid the flames of perdition, and looks you full in the face, with a horrible look of recognition, what will you feel? what will you say? what will you do? The fire that is scorching you, and that is around you like a blazing, shoreless ocean, will be ill to bear; the worm that is gnawing at your heart will be ill to endure; the thought that you are irretrievably lost will be agonising; but *that* look from *her*, when you meet, will be worse—that look will pierce your soul with unquenchable fires. Her first words to you will be, "Oh, I would not have been *here*, if I had not met you in the world above!" That sentence will echo in the chamber of your memory for ever. Man of the world, think of this in time!

The recognition of friends will be an element of woe to you too, who are occupying, in the providence of God, the awfully responsible position of parents; who are making shipwreck of your own souls, either by a life of sin, or by a life of carelessness about religion; and whose example, in addition, is leading your children along with you in the broad way that conducts to eternal death.

Image the time when you and your children meet on the other side of the veil; when your everlasting position in the place of woe is fixed, and your "Life in Hell" is begun. The world is left.

Time with you is over. You and your lost children are met, and you recognise them, alas! too readily and unmistakably. Tell me, if you can, what your feelings will be when one of your children, meeting you for the first time in your doleful prison-house, and in a blaze with all the unquenchable flames of perdition, weaving a canopy of woe around him, will accost you with a voice tremulous with the horrors of inexpressible woe,—"O father, why did you not tell us about this in time, that we might not have come into this place of torment? Your example upon earth led to ruin both me and my poor brothers, who are screaming yonder;—the rich man in hell felt that his relationship as a brother was not broken off by entering eternity. Oh! you lived upon earth as if there had been no God, and we began to think that there could be none. We heard you speak about hell and damnation recklessly and thoughtlessly, till we began to imagine the whole thing a mere jest. Would to God we had never been born! Would to God we had never been intrusted to your up-bringing! Would to God we had never been in your home! Would to God we had never seen your face! We cannot bear this agony. But, alas! alas! we cannot flee from it. The gates are shut; our prison-walls are too high to scale. The chain of misery that binds us here is too strong to break. Woe, unutterable woe, must now be our portion."

Careless father, take warning in time. You will know your children, and recognise them when you meet them in a lost eternity. Such a recognition will be to you an element of the most poignant sorrow for ever!

CHAPTER XIV.

ELEMENTS OF JOY TO FRIENDS MEETING IN HEAVEN—(*continued.*)

YOUR recognition of your friends, however, when you meet them in heaven, will be an element of everlasting joy to you who are the people of God. Your acquaintanceships, your companionships, formed now upon earth, will not be broken off for ever at your death. They will be recommenced and perpetuated in the better world.

A WORD TO MINISTERS.

I address you who are in the ministerial office. Your position in the world and in the Church is one of very great responsibility, and momentous issues are depending upon the duties which you are privileged to discharge. You are Christian ambassadors sent forth by Him who is upon the throne of His glory, and who is reigning in His grace to save, that you may make to all men the offer of salvation through the finished work of Christ, redemption through His blood. Has the God of your salvation not blessed you with the gale of what is termed a successful ministry. Have you, in return for your prayers and anxiety for the salvation of your people, met their coldness and scowl, their heartless absenting themselves from the public ordinances of religion? Have your people treated you as the Jews treated your Saviour before you? Have they reviled you, spoken despitefully of you, and have some of them gone back so as to walk no more with you? Be not discouraged in the work of your Lord and Master. Judas and many others went back from Christ, and walked no more with *Him*. Many fickle and false-hearted Christians deserted the ministry of Paul and other apostles. Be not discouraged. Your church is not so well attended, it may be, as you could wish. Heaven is not so well filled as Christ desires. Labour on; pray without ceasing; there may and there will be some who will meet you in heaven, and will give you the joy of knowing that your ministry, unblessed to many who closed their hearts and scowlingly turned away from you, was blessed for the salvation of *their* souls. They will welcome you as their spiritual father when they meet you in glory.

Has the great Head of the Church blessed you in the discharge of your ministerial duties? Have *you* had a season to your own soul, and, it may be, to some, to many of your people, of spiritual refreshing from the presence of the Lord, and from the glory of His power? Is there one, are there many, who now look to you as their father in Christ, who are as seals of your ministry, gems in your Redeemer's crown, the children of God, the heirs of glory? You feel these converts to be the source to your souls of great spiritual comfort here, and the cause of an ever-glowing gratitude to Him who is the God of your and of their salvation. You will rejoice over these trophies of Christ's grace and of your ministry for ever. The apostle Paul looked forward to the time when he should meet those who were converted by his agency at the judgment-seat of Christ, and says, "For what is our hope, or joy, or crown of rejoicing? Are not even ye in the presence of our Lord Jesus Christ at his coming?" Would the apostle rejoice over these converts? Would their presence and appearing be an element of gladness to his soul in the great day of the Lord? And will he not rejoice over them, and that through eternity, when he rises along with them from the judgment, enters heaven, associates with them there, with the full knowledge on his and on their part that he was the instrument upon earth of bringing them to a knowledge of the truth as it is in Jesus, and through whom they had been saved? It will be so with you also, ye ministers of Christ, when you rise to heaven, and meet there in full recognition those whom you led to Jesus, and were instrumental in saving by your ministry upon earth. Assuredly this recognition will be an element of joy to your glorified spirits. Christ had a joy set before Him, and which He now possesses in heaven, —the joy of saving a great multitude of the human family, by His sufferings and death, to share heaven with Him for ever, and to rejoice in His presence there. This joy, in a subordinate degree, will be yours. Those who listened to your voice upon earth, and fled to Jesus for salvation, will be to you a crown of joy and of rejoicing in glory. "They that be wise shall shine as the brightness of the firmament, and they that turn many to righteousness as the stars, for ever and ever." Ministers of the gospel, do not forget this high truth in your intercourse with your people before God! Do not labour for souls merely as those who must give an account. Labour for souls actuated by the constraining influence of the love of Christ, and ever remembering that their salvation will add to your happiness throughout eternity in heaven.

A WORD TO COMPANIONS.

You imperceptibly exert an influence over each other's characters, either for good or for evil. In your present intercourse, keep this before you, that you will know each other when you meet in heaven, and remember there all that is passing betwixt you here. Act now with this great anticipation in view. See to it that your present intercourse is such—in your walk with God, in your holy life, in your heavenly conversation, in your religious interchange of your views upon spiritual and divine things—as you may expect will be perpetuated in glory, and carried on through eternity, in the presence of your God. Thus your meeting in heaven at your death, and recognition of each other before God, not as associates upon earth, but in the higher and holier companionship of heaven, will be an element of joy to your souls, and that for ever.

A WORD TO BROTHERS AND SISTERS.

You are friends, and you have become acquainted with each other in the most interesting of all circumstances. You are not merely the inhabitants of the same world, and equally members of the human race,—you have been born successively, it may be, in the same home, and are the members of the same family; the same fond parents are watching over you in love. You are equally dear to their warm and tender hearts; you kneel morning and evening at the same altar in family prayer; you worship God publicly in the same church; you sit or kneel in love at God's altar in holy communion: and in your present state of grace, you are making preparation for the same heaven, where you are yet, as the children of God and believers in Christ Jesus, to meet, to sing the same song, to dwell for eternity in the same home. You know each other in the Lord here. When you leave the earth and enter heaven, you will recognise each other before the throne of His glory above, and before the unveiled face of your glorified Redeemer. When you thus meet, you will know each other, and remember in the skies the whole of the life you are spending now together, and all that is passing betwixt you in your intercourse here.

Will, then, every word you are uttering to your brother and sister be remembered by you when you meet in your Father's home above? Will every action you are now performing towards them be fully recollected and pondered over when you meet in a holy heaven? Will every look of love and scowl of petulance be fully in your view when you see your brother yonder, and look into your sister's face, radiant with the light of eternity, and glowing with the emotions of heavenly love? Do you believe this? Tell me, then, *how* you should spend life together here, in the prospect of it? Happy ye whose present intercourse in your parents' family, your union, your love, your religious conversation, are an earnest and foretaste of what you are to experience again in each other's company when you meet in heaven! Your prospect is delightful—your meeting above will be unmingled gladness. O Christian sister, Christian brother, see that your present intercourse here be the loving *symbol* of what you will enjoy when you *meet* in yon glorious home on high!

A WORD TO PARENTS.

Ever remember that your present opportunities of leading your children into a knowledge of the truth as it is in Jesus, will soon pass away. You may be taken from them, or they may be taken from you. Oh, whilst still with them in the same home, whilst they are still under the influence of your example, and within the reach of your voice, do not let precious opportunities pass away unimproved. Speak to them about their lost condition by nature, and of their consequent need of the great salvation that is in Christ Jesus. Tell them what God has done to save them. Tell them about the love of Jesus to children, that He wishes them to come to Him, that He is able to bless them. Speak to them about heaven as a home; and tell them how happy you will be to meet them all there, and to spend a joyful eternity with them in your heavenly Father's presence. Pray, oh, pray for their salvation at the family altar, and in secret, with the fervour and unction which the hope of meeting them in heaven, and knowing them there, naturally inspires. Tell them how happy it will be, when met yonder, to advance with them into God's unveiled presence, with the joyful exclamation upon your lips, "Here am I and the children whom thou hast given me." Christian parents! will this meeting at last, betwixt you and your children above, when life with you is over and earth is left, not be an element of joy to you there? Assuredly it will!

Image the effect which such an address as the following, by the child of your love, will have upon your spirits, as you listen to the words truthful and sweet to your ear:—"O my dear parents, we never can love enough the Triune God, who has in His grace bestowed upon us the great salvation we now enjoy. We were once afar off, now we are nigh. We were once without God, now we are in heaven, sharing together its glories and its joys: and you, dear parents, were the instruments in His the Spirit's hand of bringing us into a state of grace upon earth. We saw you read with reverence and awe God's Holy Word; this led us instinctively to follow your example, till at last it became to us the word of our salvation, the man of our counsel, and the guide of our lives. We saw you, whilst keeping holy the Sabbath of the Lord, regularly go up to His house of prayer. We went with you to our holy Zion; we found it to be to us the house of God, the gate of heaven, the place where God specially commands the blessing; and the preaching of the gospel there became to us a savour of life unto life—the message of everlasting peace to our souls. We saw you kneel at the family altar along with us; oft and oft we heard you pray—your prayers were heard and blest, for under the firm and holy belief that God *was* the hearer of prayer, we were led in secret, taught both by your counsels and example, to pour out our souls in supplications, to pray for His blessing, for the new heart which He alone could bestow, for the spiritual and heavenly blessings that were treasured up for us in Christ Jesus; and these blessings we obtained. We heard you often speak to us about heaven, as the home of love in which we were to meet and be happy for ever together; this led us to think much about heaven, and diligently to prepare for it. Heaven is, if possible, more joyous to us, now that we have met each other in it; and, oh happy thought! we will never be parted again." Christian parents! keep such views as these ever before you whilst holding sweet and blissful intercourse with your dear children in your present home; ever remember that your loving, holy, and prayerful association with them, when blessed by God, is both the preparation and the foretaste of what awaits you, and will be yours throughout eternity in heaven.

CHAPTER XV.

SOURCES THROUGH WHICH OUR FRIENDS IN HEAVEN MAY OBTAIN A KNOWLEDGE ABOUT THOSE THEY HAVE LEFT UPON EARTH.

THE subject of this chapter is not one of mere idle speculation. It may be so viewed as to become one of the most powerful Christian motives, impelling us to present exertion in behalf of a perishing world, and to an ever-onward advance in the cause of our own personal Christianity. It may be difficult to define the exact amount of knowledge which our friends in heaven have of us who are upon earth; but assuredly they have some—nay, they have much. The following considerations may tend to illustrate this:—

FIRST,—*Our glorified friends in heaven may see us, as they look down from the outskirts of the world of glory, and thus learn much about us.*

Moses from Pisgah surveys the land of promise,

and thus gains some knowledge about it. The astronomer looks through his telescope, contemplates the distant star, and gains some information about it in this way. The mother looks down from the upper story of the house, and thus learns much about the conduct of her children playing in the court below. Our friends in heaven may do the same. Abraham sees the rich man in hell. The whole of the inhabitants of heaven see the smoke of the torment of the lost ascending up for ever and ever. Thus, by still seeing us, our friends in heaven may learn much about us they have left behind them in the world.

SECOND,—*They may learn much about us by divine communication.*

Father, Son, and Holy Spirit *may* convey, by oral and direct communication to our already glorified friends, much knowledge about us whom they have left behind in the world. There is nothing improbable in this. A sovereign in the palace, a father in his home, often make communications to those around them about things in which they are respectively interested; so may God in His palace and in His home of love to those who are around Him. The Father, the Son, the Holy Spirit is omnipresent, fills the universe, sees all and knows all,—discerns our thoughts afar off, searches the heart and tries the reins,—not a word is in our tongue but it is known to God. Our friends in heaven are in direct and personal communication with God upon the throne of His glory. This personal communication may give them something approaching both to omnipresence and omniscience. Thus may they learn much—everything about us they have left behind them in the world.

THIRD,—*Our guardian angel may communicate much knowledge about us to our friends in heaven.*

The Scriptures plainly teach the doctrine of angel guardianship:—"Because thou hast made the Lord, which is my refuge, even the most High, thy habitation; there shall no evil befall thee, neither shall any plague come nigh thy dwelling. For he shall give his angels charge over thee, to keep thee in all thy ways. They shall bear thee up in their hands, lest thou dash thy foot against a stone." "Are they not all ministering spirits, sent forth to minister for them who shall be heirs of salvation?" What is the view we are to take of angel guardianship? We are not to suppose that when God assigns us, individually, as the particular object of a particular angel's watchfulness and care, that *that* angel is excluded entirely from heaven, and from the presence of God's glory above, (shepherds occasionally leave their flocks, and ministers their people,) and remains unceasingly without intermission with us upon the earth. Jacob's vision at Bethel teaches us a different lesson. Angels are not stationary upon earth. The patriarch sees them ascending and descending upon that ladder which stretched betwixt earth and heaven. In conformity with this view, I believe that our particular guardian angel gives us a general attendance, but not an unremitting one. I believe that the space betwixt heaven and earth is often traversed by him. View this fact, and couple with it this other, that angels are the members of the same family—the family in heaven—as our glorified friends now are, and have intercourse with *them* there, as well as with *us* here; may not then in this way a large amount of knowledge about us, about Christ's kingdom on earth, and about the state of the world generally, be communicated to our friends above?

Have you friends in a foreign land,—dear parents, beloved children, brothers, sisters, who are still dear to your heart,—a partner beloved, other relatives, whom you fondly and tenderly regard? Does an acquaintance of theirs from the country of their adoption pay you a visit, who has returned for a short period to the land of his nativity in which you dwell? How do you act when this visitor is in your home with you? Do you never once think about your absent friends? Do you carefully abstain from mentioning their names or making any inquiry about them? The very reverse! They are the chief subject of conversation, and thus you learn much respecting them.

Is it not the same in heaven? When your guardian angel rises from your presence, re-enters heaven, and meets before the throne of God your departed father, or mother, or children, or other friends, will they not inquire about you—*where* you are, *what* you are now in appearance or person, what you are *doing* or *saying*, and about what God, Jesus, the Holy Spirit, angels, your glorified friends, heaven, and Christ's great salvation are to you now? Your friends in heaven may thus know far more about you, and about your personal history, than you know about any one of your friends upon earth who is not dwelling with you in the same house. Live, I beseech you, under the influence of this view. Live in the world in such a way that your guardian angel, on his occasional or frequent visits to heaven, may be able to carry up a good report about you to your friends, for through such information they will be enabled to cherish before the throne of God the gladdening hope that their present separation from you will not be long, that soon you will rise and join them in a glorious eternity, and dwell with them for ever in the same home of love.

FOURTH,—*The personal visits which our friends in heaven make to us upon earth, may put them in possession of much knowledge about us.*

I have adverted to this fact among the ANALOGIES of "Meet for Heaven." I stated the fact there merely as a probability suggested by analogy. I think, however, that there is *more* than a probability that such visits of glorified saints from heaven to this world are really taking place.

Angels are not confined to heaven. Are the glorified? There are certain allusions in the Scriptures to the contrary. Moses and Elias revisit the earth, and appear with Christ upon the mount of transfiguration. The apostle John thus speaks of a visit which one of the glorified prophets of the Lord paid him on the Isle of Patmos :—"And I John saw these things, and heard them. And when I had heard and seen, I fell down to worship before the feet of the angel which shewed me these things. Then saith he unto me, See thou do it not: for I am thy fellow-servant, and of thy brethren the prophets, and of them which keep the sayings of this book: worship God." Are any of the inmates of heaven exclusively confined to the world above? God is not, Jesus is not, the Holy Spirit is not, angels are not. Are, then, the glorified? I do not believe they are. No doubt heaven is their usual habitation, as it is this to angels; but I have no reason to believe that God confines the glorified exclusively to heaven. Analogy gives us a very different view; and the Scriptures, as I have shewn, countenance by their revelations in this the teachings of analogy. Then, if the glorified are permitted to pay personal visits to earth, what home and what family will a glorified mother and father most anxiously and lovingly visit when descending to our planet? Will it not be *yours* and *you*, ye motherless and fatherless children who are mourning their absence in your desolate home? You cannot see your friends from heaven whilst present with you in these visits of love; but they may see you, and hear your well-known voices, and walk with you unseen, and feel a deep interest in all that you are doing. What knowledge about you would you like these still fond parents of yours, when they leave you to go home again, to carry up with them to heaven? You would not like them to go away from you with the knowledge obtained by actual observation that you are living lives upon earth that must inevitably land you in hell; for they have hovered around you in company with your guardian angel, and have often seen you staggering home drunk, reeling like a ship in a storm,—have heard you swear and take the name of God in vain,—have looked upon you during the holy hours of the Sabbath of the Lord. But how did they see you spending it?—differently from those they were about to join when they went up again to the Sabbath of heaven. They saw you remaining idly and carelessly in your home, or lounging through the fields, whilst God's people were assembled in church, and joining the assemblies of heaven in His worship and praise. No! You would like them, though unseen by you, to see you reading God's Word, kneeling in prayer, going up with proper solemnity of spirit to God's house of prayer, partaking of the holy communion, walking in fellowship with those who have the fear of God before their eyes. You would like them to hear you speaking of God as the God of your salvation, of Jesus as your Saviour and new covenant Head, of the Holy Spirit as your Life and Comforter and Guide, of heaven as your home, and of the joy you will experience when you rise and meet them and recognise them in glory; for with this knowledge they will gladly rise to heaven and wait longingly and in full confidence for the time when, by God's appointment, you will rise and join them, and spend a joyous eternity with them.

FIFTH,—*The departure at death of friends and acquaintances to heaven, will convey a knowledge about us to our friends who are already there.*

It is quite natural for us to suppose this. Our glorified friends who are in heaven are alive, are conscious, remember us in the skies, and still feel a deep and absorbing interest in us. Their attention is not so engrossed with the affairs of heaven as to lead them to forget the earth, and us whom they have left upon it, mourning their absence in our bereaved home. Take a case upon earth in illustration: the emigrant in a foreign land. I address you, who are in this position. You have, it may be, dear friends left behind you in the home of your youth. Does one of them, say your brother, leave the rest of the family behind, to go to the land where you dwell? Are you made acquainted with his coming, and do you know the time when the ship should arrive? How, in these circumstances, do you act? Have you no interest in his arrival? When he does arrive, do you meet him in your home and never speak? Do you pass him silently by, and do you make no inquiry at him about those dear friends he has so lately left in the home where you once dwelt, and spent the morning of life with those who are still there? The very reverse is the case. At the time the ship is expected, with your bosom all in a flutter, you look with eager eyes and with a beating heart onwards to the far-off horizon. You wait and linger on the shore, in the expectation of seeing the ship emerge and come into your view. When this does take place, what emotions circulate through your being? The ship approaches nearer and still nearer. At last you see upon the deck your brother standing, and looking intently towards you: the ship is in the harbour, the anchor is let go, your brother steps on shore; you meet him with a warmth of feeling proportioned to the time of your separation. What is the first question you put when you meet? Joseph's, when meeting his brethren in Egypt, but changed so as to suit your circumstances—"How is my dear mother, my father, my sisters, my brothers?" And as you sit with your newly-arrived brother in your house, or walk with him by the way, about what chiefly is your conversation? Is it not much about those who are at home? Thus by this single visit you become acquainted with their circumstances and their life since the time you left them. It is the same, rest assured, in heaven. Take the case, once more, of your now-glorified mother. She has left a dear and beloved family behind her. She may learn up in heaven much about you whom she has left, and in whom she still feels a lively interest, by sight, by divine communication, by your guardian angel, by personal visits she may be allowed to make to you in your home of sorrow, where you often think about her and speak about her. But, in addition, take this case:—One of your sisters sickens, dies, follows your glorified mother. The mother and the daughter thus meet, know each other, are the members of the same family, speak the same language, have sweet, heavenly intercourse with each other, and have both an absorbing interest in you who are still in their home upon earth. About what will they speak chiefly when they meet? Will it be only about what they *see* there, and about what they *hear?* No, it will be about *you!* Thus distinct and intelligent tidings respecting you will be carried up to your mother in heaven by that dear deceased sister who has left you.

There are many in heaven who feel an interest in us, and who may in this way obtain a knowledge

M

about us, who are still upon the earth, through friends and neighbours and acquaintances at their death leaving us here and entering there. The minister may thus learn much about the people of his former charge; the missionary, about the spread of the gospel in heathen lands where he once laboured; parents, about children still in the world below; partners, about those they have left in their sorrow; children, about their parents who are still living in the home where they died.

Rest assured there is far more knowledge about us, conveyed in the ways I have mentioned, possessed by our friends in heaven, than we are apt to imagine.

Christians, mourners in Zion! so live, so act, that this knowledge, thus conveyed, may be to them the subject of delight and thanksgiving to God; and may afford them the joyous hope that you are preparing to follow them, and will soon join them in your heavenly Father's home of love.

CHAPTER XVI.

THE KNOWLEDGE WHICH OUR FRIENDS IN HEAVEN OBTAIN ABOUT US WHO ARE STILL UPON THE EARTH MUST KEEP UP IN THEIR BOSOMS A DEEP INTEREST IN US.

I HAVE endeavoured to prove in "Heaven our Home," and at considerable length, the interest which those who are in heaven feel in the earth and in its inhabitants generally. I wish here to view this interest more particularly as cherished by friends in heaven towards their relations whom they have here, where they also once dwelt. Assuredly the knowledge which our friends in heaven obtain about us, in the *ways* I have mentioned in the preceding chapter, must keep up in them an unceasing interest in us.

I cannot positively tell whether or not glorified saints, now in heaven, *see* from their thrones of light and seats in glory those whom they have left behind them in the world, and who are still dear to them in the Lord. All the redeemed who are now there were once the inhabitants of earth, where we still dwell. Here they once lived, and were made partakers of the Holy Ghost, became the new creation of God in Christ Jesus, and walked with God in newness of life; but now they have left the world, and have gone up. I cannot follow them with the upward gaze of my bodily eye, so as to see them and survey them, so high, so glorious, and so happy in their resting-place above. I cannot, with my utmost scrutiny, pierce the hidings of a glorious eternity, and look upon the great realities within. For the wisest of purposes God has drawn a veil over heaven, and conceals from the human family upon earth the present dwelling of the already glorified, the home of love in which they are now assembled in the unveiled presence of their God. God does this because a constant and vivid view of those dazzling things would unfit us for the duties of earth; and because, whilst we remain in the world in a state of probation here, we must walk by faith and not by sight. We do not see with the bodily eye up into the interior of heaven,—we do not thus behold our departed friends now there, who were once with us and visible to our eye. But whilst this is the case on our side, it does not follow that we are also hidden and entirely concealed from the downward and longing lookings towards us of our translated friends. The Scriptures countenance the supposition that the glorified in heaven do see *us*, as they stand above and around the arena of earth, and look down upon us here, occupying the position of competitors for the crown of life, and, moreover, do feel the deepest interest in us, whilst beholding the manner in which we are following them to the skies, and are preparing to join them in God's unveiled presence. "Wherefore, seeing we also are compassed about with so great a cloud of witnesses, let us lay aside every weight, and the sin which doth so easily beset us, and let us run with patience the race that is set before us."

Could we be brought to cherish, firmly and abidingly, the thought that our departed friends still see us, now that they are in a state of separation from us, and still cherish towards us the deepest interest and sympathy and longing for us to come and join them, this would rob the hour of bereavement, the chamber of death, and the lonely grave of half their gloom. The loss, the deprivation, and the feeling of separation at the hour of death *may* be felt chiefly, if not entirely, on our side. A much less feeling of change may be experienced by our glorified friends who have entered heaven. *They* may even now be feeling as if scarcely *any* separation betwixt them and us had taken place, and this the while they are looking down and plainly beholding us, and whilst cherishing towards us still the full, the warm sympathies of home and of friendship.

Even granting that our glorified friends in heaven do not see, in the manner I have indicated, all the doings of the inhabitants of that earth in which they once lived, and in which they yet have an interest, still in possession as they are of the sources of information about us, to which I have referred in the preceding chapter, is it possible, I ask, that living yonder in their world of life and of love, they have ceased to inquire about us, or to feel any interest in us? The response, I do not say of reason alone, but of the heart, is—*It is not possible!* Take the case of a dear mother in heaven whose infant child, when she died, was left a motherless babe to the mercies of the world. The mother whilst here felt a deep and tender interest in her little one, and she did not leave this interest behind her when she went up at her death and entered into heaven. In a state of high exaltation, and amid the glories and joys of the upper sanctuary, she remembers her son still. Many years have rolled over the earth since the mother and child were parted. Her son grew up a thoughtless, reckless boy. When he reached the years of manhood he entered upon a life of open wickedness; he associated with ungodly companions; he never prayed; he never read the Bible; he was more frequently in the theatre than in the house of God. But, lo! one of those events which men call chance has given a sudden change to the whole current of his existence. A young companion accidentally began to speak to him about his departed mother, and expressed a wonder whether she would now see him and feel still an interest in him. This language was like a nail in a sure place fastened by the master of assemblies. The thought of God, of Jesus, of the Holy Spirit having a deep and glowing interest in his salvation, affected him far less than the thought of his mother's continued interest in him and desire for his salvation. This vision of his glorified mother was so sanctified to his soul by the Holy Spirit, that with a feeling of remorse and past forgetfulness of God, and with the desire springing into his mind of seeing his mother and of speaking to her in heaven, and spending eternity with her, he was led to lift his voice in prayer, and to weep over his sins, and to cry for mercy through the peace-speaking blood of Jesus. This is what is now going on in that young man's home. His conversion is announced to his mother by Him who is upon the throne. What is her feeling when she is put in possession of this information? It is one of deep interest, holy joy, and ecstatic gladness that her son is now a child of God, and will ere long come and join her and live with her through eternity.

Look at this other case:—A minister is among the glorified in heaven. A once careless hearer, who remained impenitent under his ministry, is now visited by a distressing accident, and is lying mangled and in great pain upon his bed of affliction. God gives a commission to one of the angels who see His face in heaven and stand before His throne, to pay a visit to that man in his home of pain. In compliance with God's high behests, that angel leaves yon bright world where no casualty ever happens, and no night ever darkens over the lovely scene.

Follow, in imagination, that angelic messenger in his descent. With wings of gold blazing in celestial light, and with a glow of holy fervour in his bosom, that seraph leaves at God's command the throne of heaven, his angel companions, the world of glory, and descends that he may pay a visit to one of the homes of earth. He passes over cities with their evanescent and constantly-shifting population; he passes over villages with their little jealousies and local scandals; he is directing his course to yonder dwelling around which the dark cloud of affliction is now gathering. Enter with me, in imagination, into that home. Upon a bed of distress there is one now lying there who has been visited by God with an afflictive dispensation. That man lived in the days of his health a life of carelessness and of sin. He lived, as too many do, without God, without Christ, and without hope in the world—without making the slightest exertion to secure the salvation of his immortal soul. Like too many, he formerly lived just as if the world had been the appointed place of his rest, and as if he had received the permission from God to live here throughout eternity, on the condition that he had obtained the privilege from God that he was never to die. It is different with him now. He has been suddenly awakened, by one of those unforeseen accidents which often occur in the providence of God, to the perception that the world is not his home. He feels alarmed, he trembles—but what is the cause of his agitation, distress, and trembling? He now feels in the position of one who is forced out to sea in a ship that is not sea-worthy and when sailing is now dangerous. He feels in the position of one who has lost his way, whilst a dark and a starless night has thrown its clouds and its storms around him, and who has undesignedly turned his footsteps towards the sea-shore—there is a terrific storm upon the ocean, the lightnings of heaven suddenly gleam over his benighted path, and shew to his alarmed and startled eye that he has clambered to the very edge of the rock which, in towering grandeur, overhangs the yawning abyss, whilst the dashing waves and rolling, foaming waters of the sea growl in frightful and terrific moaning in the deep and dark cavern below. He feels in the position of the man who sees above him and around him the dark thunder-cloud in the sky, and whose eye is suddenly arrested by the first glare of the thunder-bolt descending to strike the very spot of ground where he stands in his stupor. That man, in his affliction, has been as suddenly and alarmingly awakened to a sense of his terrible danger, whilst in the lightning's gleam of God's great wrath he sees himself standing upon the verge of an undone eternity and about to tumble headlong into the abyss of the great ocean of fire beneath. His body shivers. His eye is streaked with red and is restless. He turns and turns, but can find no rest. The chill of a terrible fear and the deep horror of coming vengeance roll over his trembling spirit like a deluge of wrath. The careless observer might readily but rashly infer that the cause of that man's suffering is in the fire of the fever that is burning up the moisture of his body, or in the throbbing of the inflammation that is giving him such a restless and such an uneasy pillow. The seat of that man's pain and anguish and restless tossing, however, is not so much in the body—it is in the soul. That man is now brought, by God's dealings with him, to see his need of salvation, and out of the depths he is crying to God for deliverance. The burning remembrance of a thousand sins is rushing in upon his now fevered brain like the red lava from the volcano's mouth down the mountain-side and over the grassy plain to scorch and to burn. His bosom is like the troubled sea, he feels a storm upon it more terrific and more fearful than ever heaved the waters of the Atlantic Ocean, tumbling them up into their rolling mountains. That man now feels himself spiritually diseased, and he is in quest of a spiritual physician; he feels himself *lost*, and he is in quest of a Saviour—he is seeking

Jesus. He is like Noah's dove in the midst of the encircling floods of his spiritual anguish, and he is in quest of the Ark of Salvation. In the midst of the deep darkness of a terrific night, and in the midst of the rising and threatening billows of an overflowing deluge, he is praying for light and deliverance with the deepest earnestness, and is groping his way to the opened door of the ark. The Holy Spirit is descending from the Father and the Son upon the mission of that man's salvation. The Spirit, in His work of awakening and conviction, is now dealing closely with his conscience, and is now moving graciously upon his soul. Under the Spirit's operations of grace, that man passes from death into life—he emerges into the light, and joy, and gladsomeness of a new and of a joyful day—he is translated out of the kingdom of darkness into the kingdom of God's dear Son. Oh, what a joyful and delightful change has taken place in his spiritual experience! Beneath the dawning light of a new day he exultingly exclaims, "O Lord, I will praise Thee! Thou wast angry with me, but Thine anger is turned away, and Thou comfortest me." "The Lord is my light and my salvation; whom shall I fear?"

But where now is that bright seraph, in company with whom we entered that home of affliction, to see a child of God born from above, and to see the cold winter of nature, that previously spread itself over that man's soul, give place to the light and the gladsomeness and warmth of a spiritual summer? He has already left it; he has executed his commission; he has ascended, not in horror, but with a bosom full of holy joy; he has returned to his native heavens; he has entered the courts of glory, to relate there the great event that has taken place—the repentance of a sinner. Over this event heaven rings jubilee. "I say unto you, That likewise joy shall be in heaven over one sinner that repenteth." "Likewise, I say unto you, There is joy in the presence of the angels of God over one sinner that repenteth." When all who are in heaven rejoice over that man's conversion, assuredly his former minister will feel a deep interest in the great event; for this intelligence, brought home to heaven through the agency of that ministering angel, puts him in possession of the gladdening truth, that another of his hearers has turned his face and his footsteps towards Zion, and is preparing to join him in heaven.

Here is another case. Enter with me into yon home, in which a drunken father has caused such misery and acute suffering. That father makes good wages, but he squanders them thoughtlessly and recklessly in the tavern, and allows his family to pine and suffer. His poor partner long remonstrated, and tried to win him back to the path of sobriety and decency, but all in vain. Whilst his *wife and* children are in his wretched home, shivering in the cold, without fire, without proper clothing, and almost without food, often does he sit by a blazing hearth in the tavern and spend his money, which *might* do so much for the comfort of those whom every consideration should lead him to provide for and to protect. The result of his conduct is, that his poor partner is now upon a bed of affliction, and there she is dying—dying literally of a broken heart. She prays for her children, that God may protect them, and be a father to them, when she is gone; and oh, affecting sound, she prays for her husband, that the Lord may touch his heart, and open his eyes to see the ruin which his conduct is bringing upon himself and upon his poor suffering family. That prayer is heard. The children cling in their tears around their mother's dying bed. The husband looks on sullen and cold, besotted and heartless. The mother dies; rises from that home of misery to her Father's home of love in the heavens, and enters into the joy of her Lord. There is a voice in the very silence of the home where death enters, which makes the most abandoned sometimes pause and consider. The careless father hears that voice. He pauses. He reflects. He begins to feel upon his soul a heavy burden of guilt. He prays. God hears him. The Holy Spirit descends upon his soul in His quickening and life-giving influences. He passes from death unto life. He now shuns the cup of intemperance. He begins to love his children, and to care for them in the

Lord. He prays for them, that God may bless them and give them all to meet at last—a family in Christ, a family in heaven. Meanwhile, as this change is taking place in the father's conduct, a daughter, whose health has been injured and undermined by want during the days of her father's infatuation, falls into ill health, and after a not very lingering illness, dies of consumption. She bids her now dear father adieu, and lifts her dying voice in thanksgiving to God, that she can now leave him with the high and holy hope of again meeting him in heaven. She parts with her brothers and sisters. She falls asleep in Jesus. Her body returns to the earth as it was, and her spirit returns to God who gave it. She rises and enters heaven. She meets her mother before the throne of God, and makes known to her much about the dear friends she had left in her home. Almost the first tidings the daughter conveys is, "My father is converted, has become a sober man, and is diligently and prayerfully preparing to join us here, and to be with us for ever." I leave the reader to imagine the interest which this announcement will have to the soul of the glorified mother.

CHAPTER XVII.

CHRIST'S LIFE IN HEAVEN, THE PATTERN OF HIS PEOPLE'S THERE.

THE subject of this chapter is one of great difficulty. Even the very attempt to give a written portrait of Christ's life in heaven may be looked upon as something like presumption, and a meddling with those high and sacred and awful realities which we are not to endeavour to look into. If you who read are among those who think this, I ask you, Do you feel that it is presumption in you to *speak* about your Redeemer in heaven, and about the life which He is spending on high? Is not this the very foundation of all personal Christianity—a looking to Christ for salvation, and following His footsteps in the regeneration here? I do not wish rashly to pry into these secret things which belong to the Lord our God; but what I assert is, that Christ's life in heaven is not one of these. The sacred writers, in many a passage of Scripture, speak to us about it; and so far from its being wrong to meditate upon the great subject which these passages bring under our view, it would be a sin not to do so.

Do not tell me that all the views which I may form or express in writing about Christ's life in heaven, should be comprised in the exact words of Scripture, and that any attempt to add any views of mine upon the subject, in addition to what the Scriptures have said, is wrong. If this argument prove anything, it proves too much; for it proves that all who write religious books, compose sermons, or speak to each other about religion, except in the very words of Holy Scripture, do wrong; nay, it proves that the very existence of all religious books, except the Bible, is a sin. I am in the hope that a reverential view, and a realised representation, founded upon Scripture, of Christ's life in heaven, may be one of the means which the Holy Spirit may use and bless to begin and to carry on the life of God in the soul of the reader.

There is a distinction betwixt what may be termed Christ's official or mediatorial life in heaven, which He is spending with the high object of effecting our salvation, and His life viewed as the Elder Brother of the glorified—His life as one of the family of heaven. Men who occupy official situations upon earth have a twofold life—a public life which they devote to the superintendence and dis charge of their official duties, and a life which they *spend in* the bosom of their families. We should view Christ's life in heaven as exhibiting itself to us in this twofold aspect.

Christ has an official life in heaven which He is spending in the discharge of His mediatorial functions, generally towards the world, and specially towards His Church and people. As our Prophet, He teaches us by His Word and Spirit the will of God for our salvation: as our King, He reigns over all things for the good of His Church; subdues all His and our enemies, and makes us a willing people in the day of His power: as our Priest, He has offered Himself, once for all, a sacrifice for our sins in the outer court of this world, and has entered as our Representative and new covenant Head into the Holy of Holies above: "Neither by the blood of goats and calves, but by his own blood, he entered in once into the holy place, having obtained eternal redemption for us." "For Christ is not entered into the holy places made with hands, which are the figures of the true; but into heaven itself, now to appear in the presence of God for us." The Lord Jesus is thus officially appearing as our great High Priest before the mercy-seat above. He hears our prayers. He presents them before the glorious presence of the eternal Father, perfumed with the rich incense of His own atoning sacrifice. He procures for us, in answer to His intercession, the gift of the Holy Spirit. He is carrying on in our souls the work of grace, and is thus giving us a meetness for glory. He is preparing heaven to be our eternal home. He is already yonder as our Forerunner, and ready to receive us into its unchanging glory. Christ has thus an *official life* in heaven, which He is spending as the Mediator of the new covenant, and this life has a reference chiefly to us who are still upon the earth.

Christ has also a life in heaven which He is spending, not as the Head merely and Mediator of His Church in glory, but as the Elder Brother of God's great family now assembled in "Heaven our Home." This life of Christ is just an exemplification of the life which the whole of the glorified are spending above. That we may see the full force of certain glimpses given us in the Scriptures of Christ's life thus spent in social intercourse among His followers, there are *two facts* which we must keep in our view.

FIRST FACT.—*Christ possesses in heaven the very nature which His people do, and thus His life on high is the exemplification of theirs.*—The Lord Jesus at His incarnation took to Himself our whole nature. "The Word was made flesh, and dwelt among us." "God was manifest in the flesh." The Lord Jesus has carried our nature up to the throne of God; and now, in possession of universal sovereignty, He sits in our nature at God's right hand on high. A human heart glows warmly and lovingly towards us—human eyes, in their soft and piercing gleamings, and in love's warmest glance, look down from the throne of God upon all the assemblies of heaven—a human ear listens to their praises—human lips speak to angels and to glorified saints, when He who is upon the throne makes known to them new revelations of His will—a human hand holds the sceptre of universal empire—human feet walk through the bowers of the celestial paradise, and tread the streets of the New Jerusalem — human social feelings circulate in Christ's bosom as He stoops from the throne and condescends to hold high and holy communion with all who are in glory.

SECOND FACT.—*Christ is the pattern of His people in all things.*—Christ's life upon earth is the pattern of what a state of grace in us ought to be, and Christ's life in heaven is upon the same principle, and for the same reason, the pattern of His people's in glory. I have proved and illustrated these two views at considerable length in "Meet for Heaven."

SOME OF THE FEATURES OF CHRIST'S LIFE IN HEAVEN.

Christ's life in heaven is a life of rest.—Sitting is a posture of rest, and again and again Christ is spoken of in the Bible as thus exalted at God's right hand. "When he had by himself purged our sins, he sat down on the right hand of the throne of God." "But this man, after he had offered one sacrifice for sins, for ever sat down on the right hand of God." The Lord Jesus is seated now in glory at the right hand of the throne of the Majesty in the heavens, resting from His labours upon earth, His works of love, and the sufferings He endured for us whilst here below.

Christ's life in heaven is a life of action.—He is not always spoken of in the Bible as *sitting* at the right hand of God; and it is a totally wrong, it is an unscriptural representation in our minds of Christ's life in heaven, to view it as consisting entirely of perpetual rest, of unbroken inactivity. The very opposite description is frequently given us in the Bible. Christ feeds His people with the bread of life, and leads them to living waters, that there they may drink and be refreshed. "For the Lamb, which is in the midst of the throne, shall feed them, and shall lead them unto living fountains of waters." The redeemed, in company with the Lord Jesus, walk through the heavens, and, it may be, visit in a glorious retinue other provinces of God's great universe. "They follow the Lamb whithersoever He goeth."

Christ's life in heaven is a life of holiness.—Christ is the Holy One of Israel. He is the high and lofty One inhabiting eternity and eternity's praise, whose name is Holy. "For such an high priest became us, who is holy, harmless, undefiled, separate from sinners, and made higher than the heavens."

Christ's life in heaven is a life of love.—An unchanging love glows towards us in Christ's bosom. "Who shall separate us from the love of Christ? For I am persuaded, that neither death, nor life, nor angels, nor principalities, nor powers, nor things present, nor things to come, nor height, nor depth, nor any other creature, shall be able to separate us from the love of God, which is in Christ Jesus our Lord."

Christ's life in heaven is a life of variety.—It is a varied life, and so far like that which He led whilst upon earth, so far like ours in the world. It does not consist in a monotonous, unchanging sameness. We cannot read the accounts which the Scriptures give us of Christ's life in heaven without noticing this feature of it. David thus speaks of Christ as seated upon the throne—"The Lord said to my Lord, Sit thou at my right hand." Stephen sees Jesus not seated, but standing at the right hand of God, as these words shew: "Being full of the Holy Ghost, he looked up steadfastly into heaven, and saw the glory of God, and Jesus standing on the right hand of God." The apostle John, when the heavens were opened to his view, sees Jesus approach the throne upon which the Father is seated, having in the hand of His sovereignty the Book of Providence. He takes the book and opens all its seals. "And I saw in the right hand of him that sat on the throne a book written within and on the back side, sealed with seven seals. And I beheld, and, lo, in the midst of the throne and of the four beasts, and in the midst of the elders, stood a Lamb as it had been slain, having seven horns and seven eyes, which are the seven Spirits of God sent forth into all the earth. And he came and took the book out of the right hand of him that sat upon the throne." On another occasion the same evangelist sees Jesus in heaven the Angel of the Covenant, and thus speaks of His position—"And when he had opened the seventh seal, there was silence in heaven about the space of half an hour. And I saw the seven angels which stood before God; and to them were given seven trumpets. And another angel came and stood at the altar, having a golden censer; and there was given unto him much incense, that he should offer it with the prayers of all saints upon the golden altar which was before the throne. And the smoke of the incense, which came with the prayers of the saints, ascended up before God out of the angel's hand." Here is a different representation of Christ in heaven: "And I saw heaven opened, and behold a white horse; and he that sat upon him was called Faithful and True; and in righteousness he doth judge and make war. His eyes were as a flame of fire, and on his head were many crowns; and he had a name written, that no man knew but he himself: and he was clothed with a vesture dipped in blood: and his name is called The Word of God." In these various and varying representations given us of Christ in the Bible, we see illustrated the important fact, that Christ's life in heaven is a life of variety.

Christ's life in heaven is a life of high communion

and of the most endearing intercourse with not some merely, but with all who are in heaven.

What the apostle John and his fellow-disciples experienced upon earth, he and they now enjoy in heaven. They have still communion with the Father, and with His Son, Jesus Christ. Christ's life in heaven is a life of sweet and holy communion, not merely with the Father and with the Eternal Spirit, but also with angels in their glory and beauty and love, and with all the saints who shine in all the splendour of Christ's own refulgent image. This communion betwixt Christ and His people in heaven is personal, and of the most endearing kind. View Christ upon earth in His intercourse with His disciples and followers, and you see there an illustration of the higher and sweeter and far more endearing communion which the Lord Jesus now has with His people, and which He will continue to have with them for ever.

CHAPTER XVIII.

INTERCOURSE IN HEAVEN—INDIVIDUAL EXAMPLES.

THERE is such a thing as "Life in Heaven." Wherever upon earth, so far as known, intellectual life exists, it manifests itself largely in intercourse with those around who possess a similar nature. It must be the same in heaven, which is emphatically the world of life, intellectual, moral, and social. The communion of saints exists among God's children here; it is so also yonder. The life of the children of God in heaven is not spent in a state of isolation and separation from each other, but in near, sweet, and loving intercourse.

The blissful communion, it is true, which the glorified in heaven possess with Father, Son, and Holy Spirit, is the *chief source of joy* to their souls, and will be so throughout eternity, just as this communion is the chief source of religious joy to God's children upon earth. But the intercourse which the children of God have with each other is unquestionably a ***subordinate source*** of comfort to them both in earth and in heaven. Many writers in memoirs of Christians, in novels, in newspapers, in magazines, and otherwise, are engaged in describing to us what may be termed, "Life on Earth." I trust that I may not be looked upon as rash in attempting to describe a higher life, even that of God's children in heaven, the life that awaits you through eternity. I believe that Christians generally contemplate heaven too much in the mass, and as a great whole, forming of it those complex ideas which Locke has shewn to be such a fertile source of error in our contemplation even of the objects of nature around us. I hope, by individualising and contemplating separately some of the saved who are in heaven, I will be able to give a more vivid view of the world of glory, and of those who are in it, than I could possibly do in any other way.

View with me, then—by looking up and in upon the peopled heavens—two Bible saints, whose writings left to us in the Scriptures shew, that whilst upon earth they each possessed a fervent and most luxuriant imagination, and, by an instinctive attraction, we may reasonably suppose, often meet and pass a portion, not of their time,—for they have now done with time,—but of their glorious and joyous eternity, by entering into sweet and holy converse, either about their lives on earth, or what they are now experiencing in heaven. These are Isaiah the prophet and John the divine.

Isaiah:—"During this intermission of the more public worship of our God, in which we all delight so much to take a part in this high and spacious heaven, I have been pondering the views I now possess of Him, who is there so glorious upon the throne, with those I had whilst down in the world. In the year that King Uzziah died, I saw, whilst upon earth, the heavens opened, God upon the throne, the cherubim above and round about the throne, and heard their euphonious voices audibly proclaiming, 'Holy, holy, holy is the Lord of hosts: the whole earth is full of his glory.' I often obtained, in the visions I received from on high, and in the fervour of poetic piety, high and lofty views of the great and Almighty God. I saw Him walking upon the circle of the heavens in all the sovereignty of His majesty, and in all the brightness of His glory; whilst the inhabitants of the earth beneath appeared to me only like grasshoppers before Him. I saw Him in the eternity of His unchanging existence, ever the same, the great Father of lights, with whom there is no variableness, neither the least shadow of turning; whilst the generations of men, beneath the kind and pitying look of His eye, were passing away like the withering grass, the fading flower, the meteors of the night. I saw this heaven in imagination, which is now our bright and happy home, spread out gloriously, a great pavilion, for God in His Almightiness to dwell in and walk through, when the pillars of the skies were trembling beneath His feet, whilst man was in his cottage of clay crushed before the moth. I saw the stars gleaming in the pavement beneath the Almighty's feet, and often pictured these to be the mere visible outshining of the glorious hosts now around us here. The heart of man, and especially when warmed by the inspiration of the Almighty, can conceive much; but how far short, whilst I was upon earth, did I fall in my views of God, and of the bright inhabitants of His holy heaven! How glorious is God, and how full of splendour is that throne upon which He reigns in His love!—a throne of glory truly is it, that is high and lifted up. Bright is the face of God! We could not look upon it even here, were it not shining upon us in the softened lustre of this light of eternity! Loving is the eye with which He is looking down upon His great family! Sweet are the tones of that voice with which He speaks to us in the language of heaven! Great in number, shining in appearance, are the whole multitudes of glorified saints who are before and round about the throne; and of these angels, who are in their battalions of light, gazing so reverently and lovingly upon the face of Him who reigns; they have gazed thus long—they are not yet satisfied, and never will.

"I had a lofty conception of Jesus, whilst I was

upon earth, as the mighty God, the everlasting Father, the Prince of Peace, who was to become a child born and a Son given. How feeble, however, were my highest imaginings of Christ with what He now appears on the right hand of the throne of God! He is the brightness of the Father's glory, and the express image of His person. I saw the Holy Spirit as the Fountain of life, the living waters; but how differently does He appear to me now,—the pure river, the living waters that refresh and gladden heaven! Our heavenly Father conceals the great and glorious realities which we now see from His children upon earth, for yonder is the province of faith. But, oh! if I were to be clothed with my body once more, and were permitted to go down from this glad heaven to mingle again with the members of the human family, to declare to them the word of the Lord as I did of old, and to speak about the portion that awaits them here as their eternal reward; much more loftily and impressively could I portray it, both in the language of inspiration and in the words of heavenly truth, than I ever did whilst upon earth. How bright the heavens are! How glorious their inhabitants! How wondrous and blissful the portion is which God has prepared for them who love Him and serve Him upon earth!"

John:—"I join responsively in the views which you have now expressed. I, too, feel how little, whilst in the world, the members of the human family can conceive of the portion that awaits them here. I had vouchsafed to me, whilst on earth, frequent and bright views of this world of life, of glory, and of love, in which we now dwell. When the sun sets in the world below, and leaves the earth in darkness, then it is that the stars in their brilliancy and friendly shining come into view, to light the traveller home, and to guide the mariner upon his trackless voyage. I found this realised in my life. I was exposed to manifold sufferings in a sinful and godless world, for the word of God, and for the testimony of Jesus Christ. Banished to Patmos, the night of sorrow in its deepest gloom darkened over me. Then it was that, not the stars of the firmament, but the bright and morning Star of Glory, shone out upon me, illuminating my path; and this heaven in its wonders opened its bosom to shew me, for my encouragement and comfort, what we now, in the gladness of our heart, enjoy. My lonely isle thus became to me a Goshen of light, the house of God, the gate of heaven. With what an elevation of view and trembling of delight did I look up into the opened heavens! And with what a thrill of joy did I write in my Apocalypse what I saw and heard! I wrote for the instruction and Christian comfort of after-generations the gladdening views I obtained of the throne of God, of Him who is upon it in such awful glory, the bright assemblies around, which we now see filling the heavens far and wide, numerous as the beams of the sun, that gleam through the lower creation of our God. How dim, however, are the descriptions which I have given in the Book of Revelation of this glorious heaven compared with the magnificent and ravishing reality! I see now how far I came short in my description! God's people who have read my writings will see when they rise and join us here, how much grander and infinitely more glorious heaven is than the descriptions I have given in my writings about it. I saw, it is true, when I looked up, the same God upon the throne we now see here; but, oh, how dim was my perception of Him whilst yonder, compared with what it is here! I was then, when I looked and saw God here upon the throne, like a person looking at the sun covered with clouds or during an eclipse; I saw Him merely as through a glass darkly. Here I see Him without a cloud or a veil between, appearing to us in all His divine and eternal attributes. I had bright visions of Jesus in His glory, whilst upon earth; but, oh, how dim they were, compared with what He now appears to our view, at the right hand of the throne of the Majesty in the heavens! He is not only fairer than the children of men—His glory and beauty neither the tongue of man nor of angel can ever adequately describe. I often viewed wonderingly the love of God to us, whilst down in the world; but, oh, how *little* did I then know or feel of that love, compared with what I do here! I never knew, I never realised, till I entered this upper world, how *much* God has loved us. I never understood fully till I came here, what was implied in the word 'so,' when I first heard Jesus say to Nicodemus, 'For God so loved the world, that he gave his only-begotten Son, that whosoever believeth in him should not perish, but have everlasting life.' Oh, how much did Jesus love us when He left this glad heaven to suffer for us and to die for us upon the cross! I stood at the foot of that cross, and saw the heavens that are now so bright around us all mantled in night and covered with a veil of darkness! Oh, eternity will be too short to shew forth our gratitude in the praises of heaven, for the great love wherewith Jesus, who is now so bright, and glorious, and joyous upon the throne, has loved us! Oh, the view I delight to take of the eternity that is yet before us here is, that, whilst it rolls on, new and ever-gladdening discoveries of the love of God to us in Christ Jesus will unfold themselves to our wondering gaze, and be felt by us in our blessed experience."

CHAPTER XIX.

INTERCOURSE IN HEAVEN—INDIVIDUAL EXAMPLES—(*continued.*)

LIFT your eyes yet again to the peopled heavens, and behold these three glorified saints in high consultation, among other topics, upon the great subject of the *Providence of God.* They have separated themselves for a little from the congregated assemblies of angels and of saints, who are near and round about the throne. They have walked in loving converse to the outskirts of the heavenly Canaan; they are sitting in one of the Bowers of Peace that are spread so thickly over the plains of heaven, and beneath the shade of the overhanging trees, which are above them and around them all in a sparkle and gleam, as if their leaves were so many galaxies of stars. One of them is leaning lovingly upon the bosom of the other. Their eyes are again and again directed towards the great abyss that is stretching before them and beneath. Hell is full in their view in the far-off distance, and their hands are occasionally lifted and pointed in the direction in which it lies. These are Abraham, Lazarus, and Job.

Abraham:—"I often meditate with delight here upon the doctrine of the particular providence which God exercises over His great family both in heaven and upon earth. My life in the world below was a continual illustration of it. I literally walked with God, for I saw Him who was then invisible to my bodily eye, but who appears to me so glorious now. I endeavoured in all things to let faith have its perfect work. My great anxiety before my God was ever the diligent performance of every appointed duty, and strict obedience to His word. At God's command I went out from my country and from my father's house, not knowing whither I went; but I knew that God was leading me by the hand. The covenant was mine, and a great promise of future blessing was made to me and to my posterity. That promise, to all human appearance, could not be fulfilled; for I had no male issue in the line in which the blessing was to descend; still my faith in the promise never failed. And when Isaac was born, and had grown up, and around whom my brightest hopes were clustering, how trying was the command that came out to me from God, that I was to take my son, my only son, and offer him as a sacrifice upon a mountain which God was to point out to me! I obeyed; but

I felt the command a hard one. I laid Isaac bound upon the altar; I took the knife, whilst my arm trembled and my hand shook; I knew that obedience was better than sacrifice, and with one blow I was prepared, so far as I could see, to frustrate the great promise made to me, to Isaac, and to our posterity, 'That in thee and in thy seed shall all nations of the earth be blessed.' My faith, however, never once staggered. I knew the God of truth had promised; and I never once hesitated to give obedience when I had from the heavens in which we are now, and from the mouth of God, the distinct command. How glad I was to receive Isaac back! But whilst my faith was strong in the promised earthly inheritance, and in a promised Saviour, it was strong and unshaken, also, in the promise of the heavenly inheritance we now enjoy. Had I believed merely in a *general providence* exercised by God over the world, I never could have placed this unshaken faith in His promises. If I had merely believed in God exercising a *general providence* over the children of men, I never could have looked up to Him as my God in covenant. God in covenant is God exercising a *particular providence* over His children, whom He has taken into covenant, and to whom the promises contained in the covenant are personally made. It is this belief in a particular providence that strengthens faith, animates *hope,* kindles love, and is oil to the wheels of obedience. I knew, during all my wanderings upon earth, that my heavenly Father was watching over me, His shield was around me, and that in all my ways I was upheld and guided by the right hand of His righteousness. What a support this view gave me at the hour of my death, when I was 'gathered to my fathers' here! I walked with God during my life in the world. He gave me victory over death, and walked with me as my guide through the dark valley, and ushered me triumphantly into this world, His kingdom and glory. We cannot look around us, even here, without seeing the evidences of God's *particular providence.* The different ranks among the angels —the place in the scale of being they respectively occupy—the different degrees of glory among the saints of God—the intimate communion and fellowship which we have with Father, Son, and Holy Ghost—all our names in the Lamb's Book of Life —all our portions and our experiences here determined by a God of infinite wisdom and of infinite love,—all bear witness that God is overshadowing us by His covenant presence, and is watching over us with more than a father's care, and with more than a mother's tenderness. But whilst God is thus watching with a *particular providence* over every member of His whole intelligent family, His providence is not a cold, sullen, unpitying, and predestinating Fatalism, blindly dominating over the members of the human family. Those who are now imprisoned in yon awful world of fire—the smoke of whose torment is ascending up for ever and ever—voluntarily, as free agents, chose the pleasures of sin for a season, knowing distinctly that the result would be the pains and agonies and cries of a lost eternity. Is it not the arrangement of a particular providence that has led God to place yonder awful hell full in the view of this glorious heaven?—for the sight of what the lost are enduring makes the praises of heaven louder and sweeter. This sight, also, is one of the subordinate means by which the inhabitants of heaven are established in their eternal righteousness and obedience,—it is in the Lord Jesus, our new covenant Head, that we are to be supremely established here in the covenant of our God for ever. I see the rich man weltering in a sea of liquid flame: the roaring and unquenchable fires of damnation are blazing around him. He deliberately, and as a free agent, chose his eternal portion. I hear his cry for help. Oh! if he had cried as earnestly whilst down in the world, at a throne of grace, he might have been saved, and might have been joining us here in the songs of heaven, instead of screaming yonder for help, and all in vain. Oh! it is a terrible thought, that even a God of mercy, whose love is so great, and whose compassions are infinite, who has all power in His own hand, and can do as He will, cannot listen to his cries, cannot send him help, and cannot save him now. Sad is the sight we here look upon. Whilst he is asking for a drop of water to cool his tongue, his thoughtless brothers are listening to the music, are engaging in the dance, and in a life of utter godliness upon earth are preparing to join him in the midst of his woe. What cause have we to bless the God of our salvation, and to join in His praise with all the redeemed in this glorious eternity, that He has visited us with such a great salvation!"

Lazarus:—"It is the view of the *particular providence of God* that is the chief solace of His people in their afflictions upon earth, and that is an unceasing and ever-flowing fountain of joy to us who are up here in heaven. I felt this view of my God in His holy providence with me to be refreshing to my soul, when, in a state of disease, and with the infirmities of old age heavy upon me, I was heartlessly cast down at the rich man's gate,—then he was happy, and I was in distress; now he is miserable beyond description, and I am so happy in your bosom. Not a murmur escaped my lips, for I saw that it was my Father's will that I should so suffer, and He supported me and comforted me by His grace, whilst in the furnace of poverty and pain. Bright were my hopes whilst lying an outcast, cold, cheerless, and in great affliction, encircled by the darkness of a dreary night. I looked up from the cold gate, and saw the gates of glory opening to let me in, and give me possession of this world of light and of joy, where there is no night, and no inhabitant ever says, 'I am sick.' Whilst dying, I knew that eternal life was awaiting me here. I turned away from listening to the music in the rich man's dwelling, looked up, and, oh, how refreshed my spirit felt when I heard the echoings of the heavenly praise, that rise so often to our heavenly Father before His throne, falling upon my dying ear! The thought of God's particular providence over me was like the balm of Gilead to my soul, as I looked upon the angels hovering around me, so bright, so beauteous, and so loving, whom God in His care over me had sent down from this rejoicing world to bear me home. He sent them down to the gate where I was lying, and suffering the pains of dissolution. He sent them for *me*. Joyful did I feel when I left the darkness and sorrows of earth behind, felt myself surrounded by the light of heaven, and saw that I was safely landed where the wicked cease from troubling, and the weary are at rest. How thoughtless are the wicked and the godless rich in the world below, who barter away a short life of sin for an eternity of woe! Had I been rich, I *might* have forgotten my God too; but I was poor and homeless, and I sought God to be my friend, a portion above the skies, and diligently prepared for this happy home. My cry for help was unheeded by the rich man when smiling in his gaily-lighted hall, and handing his partner to her seat; he heard it, for he looked out, but he turned away. His cry reaches us here, but, ah! we cannot help him; the gulf between effects our eternal separation; no aid, not even a drop of the soothing waters of life, can be conveyed to cool his tongue."

Job:—"*My* whole life upon earth was a continuous illustration of God's *particular providence* over me. God blessed me for a season, and showered down upon me riches and honours. I was happy in my family and friends. A sudden and terrible reverse, however, came. My riches took to themselves wings and flew away, like an eagle to the sky. My ten children met in their brother's house, healthy and happy, to keep his birthday. How sadly that day closed! A whirlwind, careering along the desert, moved in its terrific fury onwards to the dwelling where they were met, reached it, encircled it, and in a moment it was a mass of ruins, and all my dear children lay beneath, bleeding, mangled, dead! Oh, how sad I felt when I stood in the darkness of that dreary night, at that fallen home, and saw that all my family stars of comfort had suddenly left the firmament of life! Not even one child was left me, whose smile might, even then, have been like a solitary star in the sky, beaming out upon the path of the benighted traveller to light up the gloom of my sore desolation. Then it was I poured out my agonised soul before God in the words—'Oh that I were as in months past, as in the days when God preserved me; when his candle shined upon my head, and when by his light I walked through darkness; as I was in the days of my youth, when the secret of God was upon my tabernacle; when the Almighty was yet with me, when my children were about me.' My health departed; my integrity was impeached. Even then I firmly believed in God's *particular providence* with me. I looked above the human agents who had so wickedly and so heartlessly despoiled me. I saw God in all that had befallen me. Full of this view, I was able resignedly to say—'The Lord gave, the Lord hath taken away; blessed be the name of the Lord.'

"Often do I reflect up here upon one great error which individuals down in the world of probation cherish, who have perfectly right views in other respects, about the particular providence of God—*that the individual who suffers greatly must be a great sinner.* Oh, what I endured in my deep affliction, when I found all around me cherishing this mistake, and looking upon me as a great sinner, because I was a great sufferer! What a defence I would have had, and what a comfort I would have experienced, had my Redeemer's humiliation taken place before the night of adversity darkened over me! I could have triumphantly pointed my accusers to the *great fact,* that the Son of God most high was a great sufferer—the greatest the world ever saw ; and yet He confessedly *was* and *is* the Holy One. He sacrificed the riches of this glorious heaven; went down to the sorrows and poverty of earth; had not yonder a home of His own to dwell in. His friends forsook Him. His enemies, many and cruel, hated Him without a cause; persecuted Him who had visited them to save them; and nailed Him at last to the cross, where He hung beneath the darkened and affrighted sky, a spectacle of woe, in the sight of earth and of heaven. My sufferings were light and easy and short, compared with His.

"But Jesus had not gone down from this glorious heaven to suffer upon earth, and thus I could not appeal then in my own vindication to the Father's dealings with the Son of His love. My life appeared, even to myself, a great anomaly,—suffering so much, yet my conscience still bearing witness within me, that whilst not pure, I was guiltless of the great transgression, yea, was comparatively innocent. My friends, who came to comfort me in my sorrow, unfortunately for me were carried away with the mistaken ideas of the multitude, and thus their conversations with me, instead of administering comfort, gave me additional pain. They forgot that, in the world, God places His children in a state of probation, and that the punishment and the reward are withheld till they enter eternity. They also forgot that God appoints sufferings to His children in the world, not in anger but in love, as one of the means in the hand of the Spirit of advancing their sanctification and meetness for glory. They also forgot that God often lays sore affliction upon His own, to shew to a thoughtless and careless world what His grace can do for them; making darkness light, the bitterness of trouble sweet, the chamber of distress the house of God and the very gate of heaven: thus often, and often, God afflicts His people for the good of the wicked around them. Oh that the careless would learn to lay this great and often-forgotten truth more to heart! *They* are the cause! The wish to awaken them, and to do them good, leads God to make the afflictions of the righteous so many and so severe. What a relief I would have had in my sorrow, if in the season of my sufferings I could have looked up to Jesus, in our nature, as He is now, upon the throne with God, sharing my sorrows, and sympathising with me, with a brother's love! Oh, I had not this comfort, which all in affliction upon earth now enjoy! I could only look up to God as a God of justice; and I knew that in due time He would assert mine innocency, and put my accusers to silence; and so He did. I never hear His voice up here in heaven, but I remember the feelings that streamed through my bosom when He appeared and spake to me from the whirlwind, turned my captivity as the streams in the south, and caused the day of returning prosperity again to dawn upon me! Oh, how differently do I feel when God speaks to me here! What joy circulates through my soul when He condescends to converse with me personally, as He does with every angel and every glorified saint, from the calm and peaceful and joyous serene of His own high and gleaming throne!"

CHAPTER XX.

INTERCOURSE IN HEAVEN—INDIVIDUAL EXAMPLES—(*continued.*)

LOOK up again upon the peopled heavens. View with me, for a little, yon two glorified, and, withal, venerable-looking saints, that you may, by faith, see walking together near to the foot of yonder mountain of glory, upon the sides of which you behold clustered, here and there, bright groups of the redeemed, also walking together in love. There is above them a sky of softened blue; not a cloud dims its calm face, sweet in its serenity! The balmy air of heaven is blowing gently from the hills of celestial bliss, and is fanning refreshingly their cheeks, where immortal youth and beauty bloom; whilst peace has established its throne in their bosoms, and there love has taken up its abode. Their eyes are resting, with the holy gratitude of a heavenly delight, upon what they see around them in heaven, whilst, by their occasional look away in the direction where the earth is rolling in its orbit, it is evident their thoughts revert at intervals to the past, whilst speaking to each other about what they now enjoy in heaven. These are Moses and Elias.

Moses:—"I feel a delight in often comparing the 'Life in Heaven' which I now experience, in its rest, its peace and calm, with the wanderings, the toil, and incessant anxiety which I had whilst in the world. From the time when I received the Divine command at the mount of Horeb, sending me forth upon the mission of delivering my brethren the Jews from the bondage of Egypt, I had but little rest. I knew the eternal God, whom we now see so glorious upon the throne of heaven, was my refuge, and that underneath me were the everlasting arms; still, through a natural diffidence, weakness of faith, and slowness of speech, I trembled at the thought of whom I was to meet, and what I had to go through. What a fever of anxiety I was in when the ten plagues, sent by God in His anger, passed successively over the land of Egypt! I cannot describe what I felt that night, when the angel commissioned by God was to spread his wings of death over Egypt's slumbering families! I saw the evening sun set, and pass away over the lowering western horizon. I knew that the angel of the Lord was preparing to leave this heaven upon his mission of wrath. I well understood that by midnight that angel would have commenced his death-march over the land, and that a great bereavement was about to descend upon its families. I remember with what emotions I and my brother Aaron, Miriam, and the other friends who were in our house, killed the paschal lamb, took the hyssop, dipped it in the blood, and sprinkled the door-posts and lintels with it. To the eye of sense little apparent security could be effected by these splashes of blood upon our homes; but we knew that God had appointed this as the means of our security; and we knew also, that what He appointed was done in infinite wisdom, and thus silenced in our bosoms the whisperings of doubt and of unbelief. To the eye of faith the blood of the paschal lamb foreshadowed Christ's blood, and the deliverance we have obtained by it. I looked up, as the evening was setting in, upon the face of the sky; all was calm; not a lowering cloud betokened the coming danger and the night of wrath, when a terrible blow was to be struck. I looked upon a number of Egyptian children playing around our dwelling. Several of the eldest of the families were among them, and to these it was their last gambol; in a very brief period they were numbered with the dead. We shut the door, and remained within, but sleep did not visit our eyes that night. We talked about the newly-instituted ordinance, and about the great deliverance which the God of Israel was soon to effect on behalf of His people. The hour of midnight came. We knew that we were safe, but we *felt for* the families of the land. The silence of the grave spread around us in our home. Our very breathing seemed, as if by mutual consent, hushed into a dead calm. Our very hearts stood still, when suddenly a sound was heard, it was a muffled, soft, passing sound, like the waving of a wing. A loud scream of lamentation, in its commingled wailings, rose around us. It rose from Egypt's mothers and sisters stooping over their dead, frantically clasping them in their arms, for the blow was struck, and they were gone. That cry of sorrow seems echoing even here, in this glorious heaven, through the chambers of my memory. How glad I felt when the morning dawned, and the tribes of Israel began their march! for with a mighty hand, and with an outstretched arm, God had delivered His people.

"I often recall here our trials and sufferings in the wilderness,—like the mariner in the haven, looking back upon the stormy ocean he has left, or the pilgrim in his home, recalling the trials that befell him by the way. Still more frequently do I meditate upon the days and nights I spent in sweet communion with my God when alone upon the mount receiving the law at His mouth. How differently does God reveal Himself to us here, compared with what He did to His people on Sinai! *There* He bowed the heavens and went down, making the clouds and darkness His chariot, walking upon the wings of the wind, and the thunders giving utterance to His voice. Oh! as the trumpet sounded long, and waxed louder and louder, Mount Sinai was altogether in a blaze, and we were trembling with fear. For a moment I quaked, as well as the others. Here Jehovah appears to us without a single cloud of darkness around Him,—covers Himself with light as with a garment,—His voice, when He speaks to us, how sweet! No one trembles when God passes by us here; no one quakes at the sound of His voice of love!

"Often do I recall our visit to earth when divinely commissioned to go down to the world to meet Jesus upon the mount of transfiguration. I never listen to the assemblies of heaven proclaiming of Jesus, 'Thou wast slain, and hast redeemed us to God by thy blood, out of every kindred, and tongue, and people, and nation,' but I recall the conversation we had with the Son of God upon that occasion. We spoke about the death of the Lord Jesus yonder; we celebrate it here in the songs of heaven. And so we may, for it is through that death that glory is rising to God in the highest, peace is descending to earth, and good-will to the children of men. That death has procured for us this eternal life which we now enjoy; and whilst we have a being here, and that will be for ever, the heavens will echo our voices as we sing with angels in proclaiming, 'Worthy is the Lamb that was slain to receive power, and riches, and wisdom, and strength, and honour, and glory, and blessing.' Yes! the Lamb that was slain, the true Paschal Lamb, whose shed blood, sprinkled by faith upon the door-posts of our hearts, has caused the angel of eternal death to pass over us, and has brought us a great deliverance, is worthy, oh! is eternally worthy, of our love, our obedience, our attendance in His court of glory, our commingled praises. 'Salvation to him that sitteth upon the throne, and unto the Lamb, for ever and ever!'"

Elias:—"I, too, often recall the past, whilst enjoying, in this heaven of love, my present life of gladness. The Lord, the God of my salvation, conferred upon me a distinguishing mark of His favour by exempting me from the endurance of temporal death. He did this, however, not so much on my account as to convince a godless generation that there is a reward for the righteous, and that heaven is the home of the people of God, to which they rise when they leave the earth. I spent a life of peculiar trouble and trial in the world. Life with me upon earth was an unceasing conflict with a wicked and backsliding people. I lived in evil times. I saw the love of many waxing cold, and iniquity abounding on every side. I saw with alarm and grief the breach which sin was making betwixt the God of Israel and His people. I stood in the breach, tried to stem the floods, and to bring back my deluded countrymen to the paths of righteousness and peace. But it was all in vain. I had to flee for my life; and often do I remember my rash wish and prayer when in the wilderness, that God would allow me to die, and thus escape the sufferings and sorrows I saw before me and awaiting me. My God mercifully refused to grant me my wish. Often in love God does this to His people. He who sees the end from the beginning sees that a refusal made to some supplicated blessing is the greatest favour He can confer. This ought to teach His people upon earth submission to His will, and faith unwavering, trusting faith, in His guidance. I found that God's refusal of my request was a blessing to me, for, instead of appointing me to die, He took me up into this heaven ot life without tasting of death.

"Oh, how commingled and overpowering were my feelings, when leaving time to become a passenger along the great ocean of space, up into this glorious eternity—when leaving the earth to rise and enter this heaven of life, friendship, and love! I looked down when ascending, and saw Elisha lifting his eyes after me with an expression of deep sorrow upon his face. I waved my hand for his encouragement, and let my mantle fall. I looked down—like the emigrant gazing back upon the receding shore—upon the earth which I was leaving in company with my angelic attendants, my soul glad with the jubilant hope that I was so soon to be in this heaven where we now happily dwell, to see its glories and to share its joys; and yet I felt at the same time a passing cloud of sorrow sailing over the firmament of my joyful anticipations, at the thought of leaving so many behind me in the world whom I loved with an unabated love. The earth at last disappeared from my view. We passed the great, bright sun in our journey upwards, and the forest of stars, that gleamed like so many outstanding lamps in front of the gate of heaven. Oh, I well remember the thrill of joy that shot through my being, when, still seated in the chariot of fire and continuing to ascend, I saw heaven, the great world of life, come as if sailing in its glory, full into my view, and heard the sweet roll of voices above me, singing, 'Salvation to Him that sitteth upon the throne, and unto the Lamb for ever and ever!' Oh, what a start of holy surprise I felt when, first ushered into this great world, I beheld its vast assemblies in their robes of white burst upon my view! When I first saw God exalted upon His throne in all the brightness of His glory, I felt the blaze of His splendour so great, that in my excess of joy, it gave me something like pain. What an effect habit has! I can now, with the rapture of an ever-increasing delight, look upon the face of God, like the eagle looking upon the sun in the world below, and my bodily eye never blanches, and I can listen with the emotions of the most unmingled joy to His voice when He speaks to me here, in the tones of love and in the language of heaven. How differently I felt when God spoke to me whilst down in the world, and the first time He spoke to me from the throne after my arrival here!

"I well remember our first visit to Tabor. Ah,

we felt as if heaven had suffered something like an eclipse, when Jesus the Son of the Highest left it and went out from us, and down into the world to become a child born and a son given! How joyful did I feel when the Father, in His sovereign disposal with us here, selected us to go down, as the representatives of the Law and the Prophets, and give the testimony of heaven, in the presence of the chosen disciples, to the great doctrine that Jesus is the Son of God, and through His decease is the Saviour of the lost! When we left upon that occasion this bright heaven, and the praises of the great assemblies around us here, I felt a thrill of gladness steal through my bosom at the thought of seeing the land of Israel again, and Jesus in the glory in which He was to appear to us in heaven, when His humiliation was finished and His ascension to the right hand of God had taken place. When we descended towards the earth, I well remember the gush of old associations that flowed over my soul, when we came in sight of the good old sun—which is to the earth what Jesus in His light is to us in heaven—which had given us light whilst we dwelt upon the earth. We felt like an individual who has long been away, when he returns and looks upon the old lamp shining at the door to light him home. When we reached Mount Tabor, how delightful I felt as I looked upon the glory of Emmanuel, His face shining like the sun, and His raiment white like the light! I felt a tremulous emotion of delight thrilling my bosom when I gazed upon the cloud of most excellent glory encompassing us around, and heard from it the voice of the Father, saying, 'This is my beloved Son, in whom I am well pleased, hear ye Him.' Often and often have we visited the earth in company, but never did I experience such commingled feelings as I did then. We talked with Jesus yonder about His death. What could we talk about? Christ's death is the all-absorbing topic of conversation and of praise here. Out of the abundance of the heart the mouth speaketh. Our heart was full of the great subject, and we spoke about it, about its nearness, its painfulness, its glorious and blessed effects. These effects we see best here: God a Father reconciled and dwelling lovingly in the midst of His family; heaven peopled with the saved from earth, whose numbers cannot be reckoned up even in the arithmetic of eternity; our nature, in the person of Jesus, carried up to the throne of God. Yonder Jesus reigns in His glory, and we are reigning in Him, and we will thus reign for ever. Well may all who are in heaven who have been saved by Christ's death from endless woe, and who are raised by it to this heaven of light, life, and love, unite their voices in gratitude in this song of praise to Him who is upon the throne: 'Thou wast slain, and hast redeemed us to God by Thy blood.' 'Lord, Thou knowest all things; Thou knowest that I love Thee.'"

CHAPTER XXI.

INTERCOURSE IN HEAVEN—INDIVIDUAL EXAMPLES—(*continued.*)

LOOK again upwards, in faith, and in upon the peopled heavens. You see near to the mercy-seat, from which God shines forth in the light and glory of His unveiled presence, the altar of incense thus referred to by the apostle John:—"And when he had opened the seventh seal, there was silence in heaven about the space of half an hour. And I saw the seven angels which stood before God; and to them were given seven trumpets. And another angel came and stood at the altar, having a golden censer; and there was given unto him much incense, that he should offer it with the prayers of all saints upon the golden altar which was before the throne. And the smoke of the incense, which came with the prayers of the saints, ascended up before God out of the angel's hand." Near to that altar, and beneath its high overarching dome in eternity's holy of holies, you see the martyrs congregated, drawn together through a feeling of sympathy arising from their common previous sufferings:—"And when he had opened the fifth seal, I saw under the altar the souls of them that were slain for the word of God, and for the testimony which they held: and they cried with a loud voice, saying, How long, O Lord, holy and true, dost thou not judge and avenge our blood on them that dwell on the earth? And white robes were given unto every one of them; and it was said unto them, that they should rest yet for a little season, until their fellow-servants also, and their brethren, that should be killed as they were, should be fulfilled." In front of that altar you see three glorified saints, separated from the martyrs, and apparently looking on with great interest as they view Christ, the great High Priest of heaven, in His splendid robes of office, offering the incense and presenting the prayers of all saints to God who is upon the throne. These three saints often resort thither, drawn together by the fact, that whilst down in the world they ministered at God's altar in the office of the holy ministry. These are Aaron, John the Baptist, and the apostle Peter.

Aaron:—"How little do those down in the world think about the sensation that is produced in this heaven of ours by the prayers and supplications of the people of God when met at a throne of grace! What a power prayer possesses! What an influence the humble, kneeling suppliant upon earth has up here! Prayer has a power over all things, for it moves Him who moves the universe and rules over it,—who is unlimited in His sovereignty, and has all the elements of nature under His control. Lo, the holy day is shining in its peace and in its calm upon the world below, the reflection and shadow of this unending Sabbath in eternity which we now enjoy! The congregations of Christians scattered over the surface of the world are met within the gates of Zion. The prayers of the people of God are even now rising to the ear of the God of the Sabbath, and commingling with the prayers of the glorified here, are ascending in sweet memorial before Him who is upon the throne! The ambassadors of Christ are engaged in their ministrations at the various altars of earth, are leading the devotions of God's worshipping people, and are, in the preaching of the gospel, pointing them the way by which, through faith in Christ Jesus, they may enter into the world of life, and join us here in the praises of eternity. Lo, Jesus our great High Priest is before the altar! How sweet are the tones of that voice of love whilst interceding for the people of God upon earth! He is arrayed in His robes of sacerdotal glory, to which mine, when at the altar in Israel, bore but a dim and feeble resemblance. The censer of incense is in His hand. He is presenting the prayers of all saints before the Father, perfumed with the much incense of His own atoning sacrifice. The peculiar and distinct office of a *mere human ministry* does not exist here. *All* the glorified are priests to God, as well as kings. *Christ alone is the minister of the sanctuary and of the true tabernacle.*

"We now see—in a way we did not do whilst in the world—in Christ's mediation here, what an important institution the ordinance of the holy ministry is to the population of earth. Oh, how infatuated are many, both Jews and Greeks, Papists and Protestants, who despise ministers, and neglect to meet God in the assemblies of Zion, that they may join in His public worship with us who are up here still worshipping the God of salvation in His holy temple! These individuals will learn, alas! when it is too late, that God loves the gates of Zion more than all the dwellings of Jacob—there He generally commands the blessing, even life for evermore — and that it is no trifle, for it is disobedience to the high will of God, and thus involves their eternity to neglect the public ordinances of religion. There are two eternities into which the generations of men enter when they leave the earth. In this eternity of glory and Sabbath of bliss around us here, God is worshipped publicly by the whole assemblies of heaven. None are here who live in the neglect of God's public worship. In the other eternity, the eternity of woe beneath, there is no such thing as the public worship of God at all. Those in hell do not worship God; they do nothing but curse and blaspheme His thrice holy name. Those individuals down in the world who are living in the neglect of holy ordinances, are not in a state of preparation to rise and join us through our eternity in the worship of God: they must, after life, enter the other eternity, and there they will find, to their horror and woe, that no public ordinances of religion exist, which are just so many wells of salvation along the desert paths of earth.

"How vividly now I see the importance and the meaning of many things connected with that typical economy in Israel which I superintended for a season! The sacrifices we offered year by year continually, were the mere foreshadowings, aids to the faith of the people of God, in that sacrifice which Jesus was to offer once for all as the Great Atonement for a perishing world, and who now appears to us in the midst of the throne as the Lamb that was slain! The frequent oblations of the body we observed, were the mere symbolic indications of the spiritual cleansing of the souls of God's people by the living waters of the Holy Spirit, whom we now see beneath the light of this glorious eternity flowing forth, the pure river of the water of life. The worship of God in the tabernacle and temple were not merely the means of preparing the people of God for heaven, but also the living representation of the worship of our God which is existing here. The assembling of God's people in such masses at the three great Feasts, was long upon earth a bright indication of the gathering together of the redeemed from all the ends of the earth into this heavenly temple, where so many, both angels and saints, join in the worship of God. The temple of Jerusalem is long ago laid in ruins. No worshippers of our God assemble in its courts now; and the time is coming when a Christian church will not be seen standing upon the face of the earth, with its spire like a pious finger silently but impressively pointing the worshippers of God up to this heaven as their eternal home. The earth is to be burnt up. But—oh, how joyous is the thought!—this temple, with its altar of incense, in which we are met, will stand for ever! Our God will be worshipped here throughout the endless ages of eternity! We will never die again! Our voices will never be silent in the praises of our God!

"Would that the veil were removed from the hearts of our Jewish brethren, who are by the judicial visitation of God scattered without an altar, or ephod, or country of their own, among the nations of the earth! Would that the time were come when our God will shine forth, by the light of the gospel and by the enlightening influences of the Holy Spirit upon their long-benighted hearts, to give them the light of the knowledge of the glory of God as it shines in the face of Jesus! Oh that

Jesus would take to Himself His great power and reign, and become to the four corners of a still comparatively dark world a light to lighten the Gentiles and the glory of His people Israel! Oh that the salvation of Israel were come out of Zion! God, however, will yet arise in His power and glory and love, and all Israel shall be saved!"

John Baptist:—"I, too, love to look upon that altar, and to view my Saviour here, who, as the Angel of the Covenant, stands so often before it; for I am thus reminded of the office I filled upon earth, when commissioned by God to introduce to the Jews their long-promised Deliverer. I feel deeply what you have expressed about our Jewish brethren, upon whose hearts there is still a veil that is hiding from their view the glory of Immanuel. I was in the world the connecting link betwixt the Mosaic and Christian dispensations. I was the evening star of the one economy, and the morning star of the other. I felt a thrill of the utmost joy in my bosom when commissioned by the Most High to intimate to my fellow-countrymen, that the Sun of Righteousness was about to arise upon a long-benighted world, that the gospel day had begun to dawn. In my preaching I dwelt much upon the doctrine of repentance, and in this I had the guidance of the Holy Spirit's teaching. I still think that many Christian ministers in preaching the gospel dwell too little upon repentance; it is *right* to insist much upon faith in the Lord Jesus as the way by which the perishing are saved, but the faith that does not result in repentance is not saving. And yet, how often does a faithful minister in this respect suffer for his honesty and fidelity! I did. I was among the Jews as a shining light for a season, and a power from on high accompanied the word preached by me. Multitudes flocked to my ministry. What a prodigious assemblage stood on the banks of the Jordan when Jesus, now so glorious in His robes of office at the altar of incense, came in His humiliation to be baptized by me! Then the heavens were opened, the Holy Spirit in the form of a dove descended upon Jesus and lighted upon Him; the Father's voice was heard, saying, 'This is my beloved Son, in whom I am well pleased.'

"My fearlessness in rebuking sin caused a gloomy night to darken around me. Herod took offence, and threw me into prison.

"I was confined in a cell beneath the palace. How unlike that palace was to this heaven of light! It was dark and damp and dismal. When Herod's birthday was kept, I heard above me the sound of music and dancing; but little did I think when listening to these, that I was so soon to die, and that I was to be put to death by violence. When the executioner entered my cell near to midnight, I was asleep, dreaming about my mother and father. I thought I saw them sitting with me in our home of love, smiling upon me as in the days of yore, and speaking to me in the words of tenderest affection, and much about this glorious heaven in which we are now met. I was looking and smiling in my dream upon the well-known faces of my dear parents, when the heavy tread of footsteps upon my stone floor awakened me. I started up, and, by the light of a torch my advancing visitor held in his left hand, I saw not only his grim and horrible visage, but a sword unsheathed, which he carried in his right hand. Before he explained the object of his unseasonable visit, I knew the hour of my departure had come. I asked for a few minutes to engage in prayer. I then, still kneeling, stooped, with my face upon the stone which served me for a seat, and said that I was ready. I felt calm, for 'the eternal God was my refuge, and underneath me were the everlasting arms.' Instantly the sword fell with a crash; I heard it; my head rolled upon the floor; my pain was over, my soul had already shaken itself free from its connexion with my body. My spiritual vision followed the executioner as he lifted my bleeding head and carried it away. My attending angels were waiting and hovering over me with their wings of love, to convey my soul—myself—up to heaven; and the last thing I saw of earth was the executioner going up to the palace, advancing to the throne, and giving away my head, as a reward for a well-executed dance. Leaving the godless assemblage, I rose, and soon, along with the companions of my journey, I entered this home of love."

Peter:—"I love also to linger near this altar, and to listen to the voice of Jesus interceding with the Father in behalf of His Church and people upon earth. That intercession embraces the world. There is no respect of persons with God. Jew and Gentile are equally embraced in the glow of His covenant love. How slow I was in learning this great and comforting truth whilst down in the world! Strange, that I and my fellow-disciples should have so long misunderstood the meaning of these plain words of our Lord, 'Go into all the world, and preach the gospel to every creature!' I was the first among the apostles to break away from our Jewish exclusiveness, and to preach to the Gentiles the unsearchable riches of Christ. I only did this after a special vision was vouchsafed to me from heaven, reminding me that the middle wall of partition was broken down, and that God in Christ was reconciled, and was overshadowing the world with His covenant regards.

"How strange that those Christians upon earth who dishonour Jesus by looking to me as their head, should adopt the dogma that there is no salvation except in their church! I was the first among the apostles to denounce such sectarian and contracted views, and to act a part the very opposite. Such a dogma restricts the grace of God, which is free to all men, as well as His Word—the conduit in which the grace of God generally flows downwards to men; such a dogma is just our old Jewish exclusiveness assuming the form of Christian bigotry. Oh that the ignorant followers of the Man of Sin would cease to look to me or depend upon me for salvation, and that they would learn to look to Jesus and to His finished work alone for acceptance with God! I have not the keys of the kingdom of heaven in *my* hand, neither has the Pope; the keys are in Christ's. And in whose hands could they be so justly or so safely placed? for in all the unrestricted glow of a love that embraces the world, He reigns upon that throne of glory, and in love He reigns to save the world."

Look up again, and in upon God's glorious heaven, where life, and unity, and love, hold their triple reign. You see the river of life flowing forth from the throne of God and of the Lamb. And, lo! upon its banks you see two glorified saints sitting in a bower of love, as much one in heart and one in view as if they had never been separated upon earth! These are Barnabas and Silas.

Barnabas:—"How sweet, and holy, and refreshing, is the communion of saints in this heaven of love, compared with what it is upon the earth. Unbroken union exists here among all the children of God. It is not so upon earth. How much is Christendom rent into sects and parties! How distressingly are Christ's followers divided and separated by names, creeds, forms, ceremonies; and, alas, often also by bitter personal hatreds! We, whilst in the world, were examples of this, and were separated for a season. When the contention with Paul was so sharp that I parted from him, you sided with him, and departed from me. We parted then in anger, and never met together again for God's united worship and praise till we met after our death in this heaven of love. And—oh, joyful thought!—we will never be parted and disunited again! With one heart and one voice we will join for ever here in the worship of the God of our salvation, and will follow the Lamb in company whithersoever He goeth!"

Silas:—"I remember often, whilst enjoying together our unity and heart-communion here in heaven, the contention that parted us upon earth. But whilst we parted from each other in the world, we did not part from Christ; I and Paul, you and John Mark, preaching the very same gospel in our separation that we did previously when united, and still doing the will and the work of our common Master in heaven. In our state of separation we were still one, for we were each one with Christ through faith, and Christ was one with us all, and still continued to bless our respective ministries for the salvation of His people. It would have been wrong in me to have imagined, that because you had parted from me you had parted from Christ. This would have been the bitterest sectarianism. You parted from us, but still clung to Christ. We did the same. This is a great truth, which Christ's followers in the world below should remember more than they do in their separations and divisions. Christians differ, separate, and form themselves into different churches, but it does not follow, as a necessary consequence, that any of the parties have separated themselves from Christ. In their separated condition, Christians should agree to differ, go on respectively with Christ's work, and thus shew to the world that they are still one with Him, though separated, for they are preaching His gospel, are doing His will, are performing His work, and are preparing to meet as one in Christ's glorious heaven here. The rivers of earth are separated whilst flowing towards the sea; they become one when they meet in the ocean. So is it with the followers of Christ. They will all yet become one in this ocean of glory and before this river of life that flows at our feet."

CHAPTER XXII.

INTERCOURSE IN HEAVEN—INDIVIDUAL EXAMPLES—(*continued.*)

I LIFT again the eye of faith, and view among the crowding assemblies of angels and saints who fill the heavens like an ocean of living glory, two glorified saints, who are standing together in their robes of white near to the throne of God and of the Lamb, and whose eyes are lifted in wonder upon Him who is upon it. That is the place these two saints delight to occupy, that is the position in which they are often and often seen. They love to gaze upon the face of Immanuel, and to speak to each other in the courts of heaven about the great and comforting truth that God is reigning in grace—a God reconciled to save perishing men. These are Ambrose and Booth. Their views of divine truth were thoroughly evangelical and wonderfully similar whilst they lived in the world; and thus it is not strange that the attraction of sympathy should lead them often to meet before the throne of God, and to enter with each other into conversation about what they now experience, compared with what they did in the past.

Ambrose:—"Whilst down in the world, I delighted to look with the eye of faith to Jesus, exalted and reigning at the right hand of the throne of God. I was so absorbed in this view—Christ's session at the right hand of God—that it was constantly like a vision of joy before my mind. But, ah! how dim and feeble and dull are the looks to Jesus by faith which His people enjoy upon earth, compared with the view of Him in His glory we are possessing here through the medium of sight! Christ, as the full, glorious, and joyful manifestation of the Father, is the great object of delighted contemplation to all the created intelligences who dwell in this glorious heaven. Angels never grow weary in their looks of wonder and of love directed towards our adorable Redeemer, and exultingly exclaim with us in the ever-new and soul-thrilling praises of heaven, 'Worthy is the Lamb that was slain to receive power, and riches, and wisdom, and strength, and honour, and glory, and blessing.

"Different indeed and dim were my lookings to Jesus by faith when upon earth from what I now see here. I saw Him yonder as through a glass darkly; but—delightful thought!—the veil is now removed! I see Him as He is! Oh, how glorious! oh, how lovely! oh, how fair He is! 'Thou art fairer than the children of men; grace is poured into thy lips: therefore God hath blessed thee for ever. . . . . Thy throne, O God, is for ever and ever: the sceptre of thy kingdom is a right sceptre. Thou lovest righteousness, and hatest wickedness: therefore God, thy God, hath anointed thee with the oil of gladness above thy fellows. All thy garments smell of myrrh, and aloes, and cassia, out of the ivory palaces, whereby they have made thee glad.' He is the chiefest among ten thousand! He is altogether lovely! I gazed upon Him by faith in wonder and admiration whilst down in the world; I gaze in greater wonder and admiration upon Him here! I love to look upon the smile that is upon His countenance towards all who are in this glorious heaven! I love to look upon the beamings of affection that light up with their inexpressible lustre His mild and holy eye! My soul becomes thrilled whenever I hear the tones of His voice of love! Eternity will be too short to carry on by sight what I began by faith whilst still upon the earth—this looking to Jesus! The eye of the child is towards its mother; the eye of the lover is upon her who has become the object of his affection; the eye of the emancipated slave is upon his deliverer; and whilst this joyful eternity rolls over us, our eyes often and often in wonder and love will be upon Jesus, who is the Perfection of beauty, the Wonder of heaven, where all, both angels and glorified saints, are so beauteous, lovely, and fair!

Oh, what a gladdening sight this is which we now possess! 'We see Jesus, who was made a little lower than the angels for the suffering of death, now crowned with glory and honour!' 'He is the brightness of the Father's glory, and the express image of His person.'"

Booth:—"How much the predominating thought in our mind, and the habits we formed whilst down in the world, continue with us up here in heaven! I was deeply impressed, whilst in a state of grace in the world, with the view of 'Grace reigning.' I wrote upon this. It was the polar star in my mental firmament. It was ever in my view. God appeared constantly to some Christians as the God of a universal and mighty sovereignty, reigning in terrible majesty upon the throne,—as the God of the Law to others, whose will revealed therein is the rule of life to the whole intelligent universe. I always delighted most to look to God as the God of grace, and reigning—not merely to rule the universe—but to save perishing men. How much I was absorbed and swallowed up, whilst upon earth, with this view of our gracious God—God reigning in grace, and reconciling a guilty world to Himself! I often meditate upon the same great theme here; but here there is another subject that much engrosses my thoughts, and that is ever before me, suggested by all that I see—'Glory reigning.' This is the world of glory, and glory is reigning here. We have passed from our state of grace upon earth, and we have entered upon our present state of glory in heaven. In every corner of this great world, wherever our eye wanders, upon whatever object our eye rests, we see the evidence that here 'glory is reigning.' This is a glorious world! A glorious God is upon the throne! A glorious Redeemer is at His right hand! A glorious Holy Spirit is acting as one with the Father and the Son, in the great work of a world's salvation! Glorious angels are in their robes of white, around the throne of God, walking the bowers of Paradise, or along the streets of the New Jerusalem! Glorified saints are in numbers that cannot be computed, filling heaven, as the beams of the sun fill the lower creation,—as the drops of water fill the ocean. God is reigning here over a glorious kingdom! All are in a state of glory that are before His throne! Yea, glory, in its beauty, beams upon every countenance! Glory, in its love, lightens up every eye! I now see and feel, in a way I never did upon earth, that what we are upon earth really determines what we are in heaven. 'Grace is glory in the bud; glory is grace in the flower.' Grace is the memory dreaming; glory is the increasing light of the succeeding day. Grace is the rose in the bud, having all its parts and all its fragrancy; glory is the rose fully blown, sweet, fresh, lovely, and glittering in the dew of the morning of eternity. Truly now is fulfilled to us the promise: 'The Lord God is a sun and shield; the Lord will give grace and glory.' Glory in its floods of life and joy fills this holy heaven, in which we now and will for ever dwell. 'Holy, holy, holy is the Lord of hosts; the whole earth is full of Thy glory.'"

Lift your eyes again in faith to the heavens; and look in upon its living assemblies. Do you see apart from angels and saints who are surrounding, in their bright assemblages, the throne of God, and in a bower formed for high thought and meditation on the works and ways of God, three glorified saints seated in calm serenity and interesting converse? These are Newton, Locke, and Bacon.

Newton:—"I often contrast the views which I have obtained of the *extent* of the works of God here with those I possessed when down in the world. From this bower of contemplation we can look upon the great temple of the universe, and what a scene of grandeur, variety, and beauty opens to our view! Even if we confine our survey to heaven, how infinitely does *it* surpass, in extent, glory, and population, all my conceptions of it whilst down in the world! I delighted in the study of astronomy, which is one of the sublimest subjects that can engage the thoughts of man; and with the rapture of the intensest enthusiasm, I often and often gazed through my telescope to see in the distant conclave of space the hidden stars, one after another, emerge into my view. As I thus beheld, time after time, the outskirts of the visible creation enlarging, and the bright works of God seemingly to multiply,

I was lost and swallowed up, not only in joy but in holy awe; for as the visible creation enlarged upon my gaze, my view of God, who reigns over it, was expanded and heightened. I felt on such occasions the full meaning of the words of inspiration, 'Great and marvellous are all thy works, Lord God Almighty.' What a mighty and glorious heaven God has created to be the eternal dwelling-place of His great family assembled here! This is by far the most glorious world which God created or made. It is to the rest of the creation what the haven is to the ocean; what Eden was to the rest of the world around it; what the Holy of Holies in Jerusalem was to the rest of the temple; what the Bible is to all other books. We cannot sufficiently adore and praise our heavenly Father, who has appointed us, in the high sovereignty of His love, to be the inhabitants for eternity of this glorious world! I comprehended much, and saw much of the greatness of God's visible creation whilst on the earth. What numberless firmaments of stars have I seen since I came here, gleaming in their expansion and brightness, that I never before even imagined were in existence! I have travelled often and often, both in company with angels and with you, and with others of my fellow-saints, the great creation; for God in His love, and for the gratification of every holy curiosity, does not confine us to heaven; and during every such journey I have seen something new, some new orb that rose upon my path, a witness of God's sovereignty and majesty; some new scene that bore evidence of His goodness and fatherly care; and have always come back to join the assemblies of heaven in their praises presented to God here, with my heart more and more inflamed with love, and my mind more and more impressed with awe, over the contemplation of His eternal power and Godhead.

"I now feel quite convinced, that just as we will never be able, through all eternity, by searching, to find out God, so we will never be able to find out the *extent* of the universe. It gives us a transcendently and mightily overwhelming view of God when we look at Him reigning, not merely upon the throne of His glory here in heaven, but also upon the throne of His sovereignty, and presiding in the awful majesty of His Almightiness over the boundless universe. He has reigned thus during the eternity that is passed; He will reign so during the eternity that is coming. What really is man, that God is mindful of him! I now feel, even more than I ever did upon earth, that I am here upon the eternal shore of existence, in the position merely of a little boy, gathering a few shells upon the beach of one of the oceans of the world, whilst the great ocean of truth is lying all undiscovered before me! But what is still hidden to us is open to the eye of God. We will, with the confidence of children, accept His hand, and walk with Him in love through the heavens, and through His great universe, and praise Him that He condescends so to love us, and speak with us, and walk with us, to shew us the wonderful works of His hands."

Locke:—"Your chief study whilst on earth, a study you are still continuing to some extent here, is the greatness and glory of God manifested in the temple of the universe. Mind and matter in its various modifications have ever been the two great subjects of study to the whole intelligent creation, and will be so for ever. Your delight even here, subordinate to the adoring contemplation of God, is the inspection of God's works throughout His material universe. The mind has always been my peculiar study, and my delight has ever been to view it in all its aspects. My subject of study is greater than yours. Mind not only created matter at first, but presides over it and rules it. The ETERNAL MIND is upon the throne and is over all. His will is the law of the universe. The soul of one saint is greater than the whole material universe; it is more like God—God is a Spirit—it can enjoy God, which matter cannot; it can actively do His will and join in His praise, whilst matter is lying passive and unendowed with intelligence at the feet of the Almighty.

"You speak of the impossibility, by all our searching, of fully comprehending the Almighty, or of measuring or walking through every corner of the boundless pavilion of space. I feel deeply the truth, that in the midst of all the light that is shining upon us even here, we are encompassed with mysteries still,—things that are too high for us. We cannot even here fully comprehend our own soul, or in what way thought is connected with the mind and circles through it, and cannot describe the law, even yet, by which feeling or sympathy flows out of one soul like water from a fountain, and flows on to another soul, like the river to the ocean. This surpasses my comprehension even here; I cannot tell how the different faculties of our soul—the understanding, the will, and the conscience—are distinct from each other, and yet all belong to the same soul, and are one with *it.* I now see more clearly than ever I did upon earth, that there is a field for reason, which I traversed much, and so diligently, whilst down in the world, and that there is a field for faith. I often wonder how I could doubt for a time, during my life below, the Trinity of Persons—the Father, the Son, and the Holy Ghost—in the Godhead. I could not see the logical connexion existing betwixt the two propositions—there is one God, and there are three Persons in the Godhead. For a time I felt inclined to reject the latter proposition, and this simply because I could not comprehend *how* these two statements about God agreed. I often here wonder at my own inconsistency in doing this. I could not *then,*—no, nor now!—comprehend *how* the faculties in my own soul, which I laboured in some of my writings to illustrate, were distinct from the soul and from each other, and yet were one in it. If my logic had been consistent, I would have doubted the existence of the faculties I laboured so hard to describe. Oh, I now see, to my delight and eternal joy, the great doctrine clearly taught both by NATURE and REVELATION, that there is but one God; and at the same time I now see just as clearly this other doctrine taught in Revelation, that there are three Persons in the Godhead, the Father, the Son, and the Holy Ghost. We seek not even here to reconcile, and to make clear to our minds by our logical reasonings, these two great truths; we receive them, we see them to be true, we do not attempt to prove them, we rejoice in them; they will be to us, whilst the joyful cycles of eternity roll over us, fountains of ever-new delight to our redeemed spirits. The fountains are not fully and clearly exposed to our view even here, but the streams of refreshment and joy from these two fountains are flowing out and reaching us,—this is the evidence the fountains are *there.*"

Bacon:—"I sympathise with the views which both of you have now expressed. I feel how much my desire for knowledge has been gratified since I entered at death into this great heaven. The glorious rest of this wonderful world does not remove curiosity from our soul, nor the desire of gaining knowledge. Angels are our companions, and long as they have been studying the works and ways of God, they still look into these things, and learn from the Church the manifold wisdom of God. Earth was our school to train us and prepare us for heaven. Heaven is now the school in which God is preparing us for the eternity of glory that is before us. I made the whole compass of knowledge my study whilst down in the world, and some great and comprehensive philosophical schemes I had in contemplation I did not live to accomplish. I found the study of nature, which philosophers had been practising, a system of mere guessing and supposing what its phenomena and laws might probably be. I introduced the system which angels follow in their lookings, and which I find even here to be the right one, of a laborious induction of facts, gathered both from experience and experiments, and from such ascertained facts collected and classified; I endeavoured to rise to a knowledge of the general laws by which nature is regulated, or rather, by which the God of nature operates and manifests His will. In the same way it is you gain a knowledge of the general character of an individual, not by guessing what it may be, but simply noticing and classifying the various actions of his life. The anatomist gains a knowledge of the human frame in the same way.

"The study of astronomy gave to one of you when upon earth a high view of God. *You* saw His unity, His greatness and glory, in the magnificence and unity of the material universe. You study of mind, in its intelligence, and wisdom, and social affections, shewed God to *you* in His intelligence,—the great Master Mind presiding over the intelligent universe; every mind was, in your view, a lake mirroring on its bosom the overarching heavens, or rather the great God who is upon the throne of glory here.

"I now see in a way I never did upon earth that God is the Source and Cause of all the unity that exists, both in the universe of matter and in the universe of mind. These two unities become one in God. All that exists has its life hid with Christ in God. EXISTENCE, in all its endless variety of *degree* and *form*, has its source in the Most High. The laws that regulate the universe, both of matter and of mind, are merely manifested evolutions of His presiding will."

Look up once more and in upon the peopled heavens. View yon three glorified saints who are walking near to the Tree of Life that grows in the midst of the Paradise of God. That tree is spreading its fruit-bearing branches over them; they often resort thither in their walks through the bowers of the heavenly Eden, and talk about the past, as well as of what their poetic eyes see encircling them in yon bright world, where an eternal summer smiles, unfading roses bloom, whilst sunshine, loveliness, and unchanging beauty appear in every object which surround them. These are Milton, Cowper, and Pollok.

Milton:—"Every time I look around me upon this celestial Paradise, I deeply feel that, in the language of earth, and even in the highest soarings of poetry, you can no more give an adequate description of what we *now* see, so as to place it before others, in its magnificence, grandeur, glory, and beauty, than you could paint upon the canvas, in living and adequate colours, the splendid appearance to those upon the earth of their meridian sun. How frosted-looking and cold would appear to the beholder the light of your painted sun? Even so the poetic picturings I have given of this heaven in my 'Paradise Lost' and 'Paradise Regained,' bear no nearer a resemblance to its living, loving, ambrosial world of glory; just as the dull and motionless portrait of a friend when you stand before it comes far short of what your friend really appears in life, with his own smile upon his face, and his own warm emotions of love gleaming upon you from his living eye.

"To what an extent does the *principle of compensation* pervade all God's dealings with the members of the human family! Both I and you, my heavenly brothers, whilst down in the world, were in our individual experiences remarkable illustrations of this. In the mysterious dealings of God in His providence with me, I was deprived of sight. Long I lamented the loss. Bitterly I felt the deprivation. Oh, what a dismal and dreary night then darkened around me, and over the face of God's fair creation! The sun, so far as I was concerned, for I saw not the least glimmering of his light, became extinguished. The fair earth vanished entirely from my view. The moon and stars no longer appeared shining out and down upon me, lighting up the dark canopy of the sky, like the sweet faces of sympathising friends looking lovingly upon the sons and daughters of affliction, when the night of trouble darkens around them. Man, with his face divine, and fairer woman, no longer smiled upon me, or, when they did, I saw them not. There is something wofully depressing in the loss of sight; for when darkness unbroken and profound surrounds us, sorrow, its shadow, falls upon the heart. Oh, what I felt and how I lamented when I no longer saw the light of day, the brightest image of God which the inhabitants of the earth behold! How emphatical and true are these memorable words of the Bible, 'God is light!'

"But how can I magnify and praise my God and Saviour sufficiently for His goodness to me in that period of my deep and dark desolation! Then it was that the visions of 'Paradise Lost' and of 'Paradise Regained' dawned in their vivid portraiture upon my mind. The vanishing from my view of things visible and temporal led me to look more to the things that are spiritual and eternal. I saw a brighter world, even this in which we are now, and a lovelier day, this day of eternal glory, than those upon which the veil of darkness had fallen, flash in something of their glory and brightness full upon my view. I no longer saw the faces of my fellow-men; but, amid the darkness of that night that came down upon me, God, Jesus, the Holy Spirit, angels, saints in glory, Eden, heaven, hell, eternity, came vividly upon my mental vision in a way I never beheld before. It is the darkness of night that brings the stars into the view of those who are upon the earth. My night brought the brighter stars of this glorious eternity that now encircles us, refreshingly, vividly into my view. Often when in my lonely, dark room, feeling as if I were the only living beam of light in the midst of a benighted universe, and whilst an unseen world was around me, I walked in thought through this heaven of glory, and round about that throne on which God is exalted and reigns so gloriously, heard angels sing, and saw them in their bright forms walking through God's great creation, and talked with glorified saints in the language which we use up here. Oh, the scenery I now behold around me, and this bright eternity of glory which I see, amply compensate for many desolate years of unbroken darkness I spent upon earth! I depicted in the language of poetry what I then saw, in the bright visions of a vivid imagination with which God had endowed me, and tried to describe in language equal to the great occasion this heaven of glory and of love. But, oh, how far I came short!

how dim is the description to the great, and living, and joyous reality of this glorious place!"

Cowper:—"I entirely and feelingly sympathise with the views you have now expressed. *You* had a long, dreary night whilst down in the world, *I* had another; mine, however, was darker and gloomier than yours. There is no night, except the blackness of darkness for ever, to be compared to that which comes down upon the soul of man when the sun of reason sets, and when even the twinkling stars of hope and of peace of mind are no longer seen shining in our sky. I was visited by God in His holy providence with me whilst upon earth, with this doleful calamity; and, ah, during that dismal night, how much was every object I looked upon transformed and changed! When I looked up and in, with the eye of faith, upon this heaven of heavens, so full of light, and life, and glory, and love, it appeared to me to be something like the great, dark ocean, when the storm comes down upon its bosom, and this whilst the murky, frowning sky—the firmament without a star—broods loweringly around. I looked up to the Great God, here so bright, so glorious. The Great Father of lights, however, appeared to me like the sun in the world below when suffering a deep and heavy eclipse. Jesus, the Morning Star of eternal glory, appeared to my eye dimmed and obscured, like the morning star on earth, nearly hidden but peering gloomily and frowningly through the veil of black clouds with which the sky often covers its face. The Holy Spirit, the pure river of water of life, appeared to me sullen, and motionless, and heavy, like the waters of the Dead Sea. Angels appeared in robes of black, and dressed in mourning, as if some of their friends had died and had been laid in a grave here. The saints in glory, as I gazed upon them, appeared to me to have become gloomy and unpleasant in form, like to fallen angels who have become wandering stars in the black firmament of perdition, for whom is reserved the blackness of darkness for ever. The faces of my friends changed in their appearance, and, to me, quite lost their light and their smile; they appeared wild and haggard, looked upon me with the yellow scowl of a deep suspicion, and with the restless, uneasy expression of some terrible fear. The horror of deep darkness descended upon me, which appeared like the plumed hearse of a lost eternity, followed by all the stars of heaven in black, and moving slowly and solemnly towards me. My position in life in my own view was this: I was walking through a dark, and cheerless, and friendless world, and onwards to a dark, lowering, and frowning eternity. How lonely and fearfully distressed I felt! But even then God gave me a striking illustration how much, in His dealings with the children of men, He acts upon the great *principle of compensation!* When the light, the day of reason, again returned to me, I did not merely enjoy once more the light of the natural sun, the Sun of Righteousness also arose upon me in His morning glory and in His gladness, upon my dark and benighted soul causing a spiritual day to dawn, and the day-star of eternal promise to arise upon my heart, giving intimation that an eternal day of light and joy was emerging. Never did the poor shipwrecked mariner, struggling among the waves on the rugged shore, with the darkness of the fearful storm encompassing him, rejoice more to see the first gleam of the morning's sun dawning, which shews him the direction in which he must try to guide the floating, lonely plank to which he with a death grasp clings, where he may find a landing above the reach of the foaming billows, than I did, when the morning of salvation shone upon me, and the Ark of Salvation bore down towards me, with its flag of peace flying, and its opened door, and the voice of my Saviour in the midst of the storm was heard saying, in calm and loving tones, 'Come unto me,' and this whilst the arms of His everlasting love were stretched forth to snatch me from my perils and fears, and I felt myself encircled and safe for eternity in His covenant embrace. Had I not been thus afflicted, I probably would not have been thus visited in a season of love. Truly can I now say, in the language of another saint, 'For our light affliction, which is but for a moment, worketh for us a far more exceeding and eternal weight of glory.'

Sweet is pleasure after pain, joy after sorrow, the bright morning's dawn to the benighted traveller; sweeter to me, inexpressibly sweeter, is the light of glory around us here in heaven when I call to remembrance some of the dark scenes I passed through during my short sojourn on earth! Oh, what a joyful thought this is—there is around us here the light of a day to which no night will ever come!"

Pollok:—"That is the reason why I believe that we experience and prize the light, the rest, the joys of heaven, even more than angels do. The possession of eternal life here becomes sweeter as we view it and enjoy it with the full remembrance of the temporal death which we so distressingly experienced in our chamber of dissolution upon the earth. Our rest here is sweeter when we look back and contrast it with our life of trial we lived in the world below. The haven appears more peaceful and calm to the mariner when he compares it with the stormy ocean which he has left far in the distance behind him. His home is sweeter and the more enjoyed by the pilgrim when he enters it and sits down in his accustomed chair in the midst of his family, after finishing a journey full of toil and of danger. This holy, loving, and peaceful heaven of ours is sweeter to us, and our communion, if possible, more blissful, when we contrast what we are now experiencing with the toils, and alienations, and separations of earth.

"I also can enter feelingly into the views to which you have both given expression, respecting the *principle of compensation* which regulates so much God's procedure in His dealings with His children upon earth. He endowed me with the gift of poetry. That gift raised me above my fellows. That gift, however, was the cause of my premature death. I died young. By writing too sedulously and ardently at my treatise upon 'The Course of Time,' I sowed in my system the seeds of that distressing consumption which terminated my earthly existence. What of that? The briefer life, the earlier immortality. The less of earth, the more of heaven. My day of faith closed; but, oh, how bright was the day of light that shone upon me when I came up and entered this glorious heaven! I wrote and left behind me in the world a treatise upon Time. Who will ever up here write in befitting terms a treatise upon Eternity? Eternity is a great subject. It is too high either for saint or angel; yea, even for the recording angel, who sits at his desk before God with the pen of love in his hand, and the *book of eternal truth* before him. We cannot describe it—no, not even in the poetry of heaven; but we will see it, we will enjoy it; and as it rolls over us in its life, and light, and glory, and love, and joy, during our intercourse with Father, Son, Holy Spirit, angels, and with one another here, it will tell its tale of love to us, open to us its new and ever-enlarging sources of heavenly gladness and unmingled delight. Thus, whilst 'THE COURSE OF TIME' with us and with all the redeemed who are in heaven is past and gone, there is now happily flowing over us, and there is still before us, in all its gladness, THE COURSE OF A GLORIOUS ETERNITY!"

THE END.

CPSIA information can be obtained
at www.ICGtesting.com
Printed in the USA
LVHW100445110522
718424LV00003B/240

9 783375 001070